The Marchioness tu[...]
able expression of a[...]

"You be quiet! Dou[btless you are as much to blame]
for this immoral behaviour as he is! Let me point out,
Forella, that no man would have come to your
bedroom unless you had encouraged him!"

Her aunt's attack was so astonishing that for a
moment Forella could only stare at her open-
mouthed.

Then as she tried to find words in which to express
her own innocence the Marquess said:

"I suppose, Sherburn, the only thing you can do in
the circumstances is to make the best of it. After all, I
cannot have my niece's reputation soiled by scandal
at her age."

Again there was silence and Forella, looking
apprehensively at the Earl, thought she had never
seen a man look so grim and at the same time so
contemptuous.

He was not looking at her uncle, but at her aunt as
he said:

"Very well, you win! I will marry your niece, and I
hope she enjoys being my wife!"

Help from the Heart

Barbara Cartland

ARROW BOOKS

Arrow Books Limited
17–21 Conway Street, London W1P 6JD

An imprint of the Hutchinson Publishing Group

London Melbourne Sydney Auckland
Johannesburg and agencies throughout
the world

First published 1984

© Barbara Cartland 1984

Set in Linotron Pilgrim by
Book Economy Services, Burgess Hill, Sussex
Made and printed in Great Britain
by Anchor Brendon Limited, Tiptree, Essex

ISBN 0 09 933340 6

Author's note

It is true that the Prince of Wales, later Edward VII, had a special way of finding the bedroom of some beautiful woman who attracted him. As the houses in which His Royal Highness stayed were usually very large, he suggested that a rose, placed outside the bedroom door, would simplify his search and prevent embarrassing mistakes.

The Prince was married to the beautiful Alexandra of Denmark in 1863, but five years later when their third child, Princess Victoria, was born, his love affairs were already delighting the gossips.

There were tales of enticing beauties in Russia where the Prince attended the wedding of Princess Alexandra's sister Dagmar to the Tsarevitch Alexander, and of seductive Princesses and actresses in Paris, which he visited alone the following year.

There the Prince led the way and inevitably the younger members of Society followed.

To many it was a very welcome rebellion from the solemnity and the worthy preciseness of the Prince Consort and, after his death, the gloom and boredom of Queen Victoria's unceasing mourning at Windsor Castle.

1

1870

Dinner was finished and the ladies moved into the large Salon with its crystal chandeliers and masses of exotic flowers.

They looked like beautiful swans with their gowns swept back into the new bustle which had just, on Frederick Worth's instructions, supplanted the crinoline.

The bustle accentuated their tiny waists, and above it their tight bodices outlined their curved breasts and seemed to draw the eye to the low *décolletage* which again had just come into vogue.

An uninformed observer might have been surprised at the sight of so many beautiful women congregated in one room if he had not known their host was Prince János Kovác.

Everything in Alchester Castle seemed to have an aura of wealth surrounding it which was inescapable.

Only one or two of the older members of the large house-party assembled there for the weekend could remember what the Castle looked like before the Duke of Alchester had sold it to the Prince.

"One consolation," a Dowager glittering with a fortune in diamonds said, looking at the pictures hanging in the Salon, "is that the Alchesters have not only been able to pay their bills, but can now live in comparative comfort since they gave up the Castle."

"My dear, can you remember what it was like?" her companion exclaimed. "Bitterly cold in winter, the walls and ceilings damp because the roof leaked! Nothing had been repaired or mended for at least fifty years! And the food was quite inedible!"

The Dowager laughed.

"Rather different from tonight!"

There was silence as both of them thought how superb the dinner had been, and how as course succeeded course the wines accompanying them had been the joy of every epicure present.

It was inevitable that everybody should extol the Prince's possessions, until they ran out of adjectives.

Prince János Kovác, who more or less reigned over thousands of acres in the east of Hungary, had come to England in the first place to hunt.

He had been so delighted with the sport he enjoyed in the Shires that he not only joined several famous packs, but had also set up a racing stable which had already begun to win the Classics one by one.

Had he been any other young man he would have aroused the envy and hatred of those with whom he competed.

But Prince János was not exceedingly popular with those who backed his horses and cheered him past the winning-post, but with the Jockey Club of which he was now a member.

Those he entertained with lavishness and generosity and acclaimed him as a true sportsman after every Englishman's heart.

That invitations to his house-parties were sought after went without saying, and he contrived, some-one said a little enviously, to pack more beauties into the square yard than any other host had ever managed to do.

Looking round the room at the ladies, whether they were blonde, brunette or red-headed, no one could doubt that if Paris himself had been present he would have found it hard to decide to whom he should award the golden apple.

All the famous beauties of the time were known to the Prince, and there was little doubt that they were fascinated, intrigued and often infatuated by him.

But strangely enough, even the most inquisitive gossip mongers of the Social World could find little to say about Prince János which was the least scandalous or even indiscreet.

That, however, did not apply also to his guests, and as Lady Esme Meldrum moved across the room to look at her reflection in one of the gold-framed mirrors the Marchioness of Claydon followed her progress with hatred in her dark eyes.

There was no doubt that Lady Esme was exceedingly beautiful in the traditional mould that was accepted by all artists of the time.

It was impossible to think that with her gold hair, eyes the colour of a thrush's egg, and a pink-and-white skin like transparent porcelain, anyone could be more lovely.

She carried herself superbly and her figure was that of a young goddess.

She had been married when she was eighteen to Sir Richard Meldrum with whom she had fallen head over heels in love.

Her parents had expected her to make a better match, but as Sir Richard Meldrum was already spoken of as one of the most promising Ambassadors in Europe, they were becoming more reconciled to their daughter's choice.

At the same time, after eight years of marriage to a

husband who was increasingly occupied by his duties, Lady Esme was looking around for amusement.

It was fortunate for her that the Earl of Sherburn should recognise her attractions at the same moment as she had decided he was without exception the most attractive man she had seen since she fell in love so many years ago with her husband.

Osmond Sherburn was rich, handsome, slightly bored with his own success, and extremely elusive when it came to a question of matrimony.

A large number of ambitious Mamas had thought their daughters would grace the Sherburn jewels and make a very charming chatelaine in the Earl's ancestral home and in the other houses he possessed.

But he was wise enough to devote his attention to married women with complacent husbands. He certainly annoyed a large number of them to the point where they longed to call him out.

But the Earl's friendship with the Prince of Wales and his position in Society made them think twice and decide that to challenge him would be an undoubted mistake.

The Earl therefore enjoyed himself as he wished and found that few women, if any, refused what he desired.

He had just had a brief but enjoyable *affaire de coeur* with the Marchioness of Claydon.

As usual he had begun to cool off first, and was in fact wondering how he could extricate himself from the clinging and very possessive arms of the Marchioness when Lady Esme came into view.

To say he was 'bowled over' would be an exaggeration, for the Earl always kept his feet very firmly on the ground.

His most ardent and tempestuous love affairs were

10

always conducted with a certain amount of discretion on his part which meant that his head always ruled his heart.

It was perhaps this more than anything else which made the women who fell in love with him aware that he was never completely their captive.

However 'sirenlike' they might be, however alluring, they could not hold him for ever.

"I cannot think why I lost Osmond," one beauty had sobbed to the Marchioness before she and the Earl had really become aware of each other.

"Perhaps, dear, you were too subservient," Kathie Claydon replied.

"How can one be anything else with Osmond?" the beauty replied. "He is so dominating, so masterful, and because one is thrilled by his very supremacy it is impossible to do anything but what he wishes."

The Marchioness had thought privately that from what she had seen of the Earl she was sure he needed a challenge.

When they next met at a house-party, at which neither of them was particularly interested in anybody else, she had looked at him with sphinx-like eyes.

She had been deliberately provocative, at the same time intriguing, inviting and mysterious, and as she hoped he had responded by being ardent and possessive.

But she had found after the Earl became her lover that her will-power had gone, and that she could no longer challenge him as she had intended.

Instead she became entirely submissive and obedient to everything he asked of her.

When she realised, and she was very experienced at the art of loving, that he was beginning to draw away, she had been frantic.

She realised then that she loved the Earl as she had never loved anybody in the whole of her life.

Her marriage had been arranged for her by her parents and, while she had been extremely gratified and delighted to become the Marchioness of Claydon, she had never found any pleasure in the more intimate moments of marriage.

It was only when she had presented her husband with two sons and a daughter, and she had taken her first lover, that she discovered passion.

After that she realised what she had missed.

Even then she had never really been in love until she met the Earl.

Then, having fallen so deeply in love that she had the greatest difficulty in not begging him on her knees to run away with her, she had realised that she was living in a 'Fool's Paradise'.

That Lady Esme should have supplanted her made it, she thought, even more bitter than if it had been some unknown beauty who did not belong to the same circle in which they inevitably saw each other almost every day and every evening.

The Prince of Wales had begun to enjoy a new freedom in the last few years.

He had gathered round him the younger and more amusing members of London Society, and certainly the richest and the most raffish of them.

He had been married to the exquisitely beautiful Alexandra of Denmark in 1863, but by the summer of 1868 when their third child Princess Victoria was born his love affairs had grown too numerous to be 'hushed up' or ignored.

Already two years earlier, when he was visiting St Petersburg to attend the wedding of Princess Alexandra's sister Dagmar to the Tsarevitch Alexander, there were whispers that he was doing more than just flirting with the alluring beauties of the Russian capital.

More tales trickled back from Paris which he visited, again by himself, the following year.

From then on his conquests, or what was described as his 'troupe of fine ladies', followed each other in quick succession.

The first of many actresses in his life was the alluring Hortense Schneider. After her there were beautiful women ranging from débutantes he saw at Presentation Balls to mature married beauties in the *Beau Monde*.

When the Prince of Wales set the pace – a very different one from what his father and mother had considered comfortable – who was not ready to follow him?

What was more, as one cynic remarked:

"Having invited infidelity, the Prince of Wales is now overwhelmed by it."

If the primrose path was made easy for the Heir to the Throne, it likewise became increasingly easier for other gentlemen who up to now had led outwardly most circumspect lives.

Indeed until the Prince Consort died they had been always liable at even a breath of scandal to be scolded and more or less ostracised from Court.

Now the barriers were down and the Prince of Wales's love affairs were openly accepted except by some of the more strait-laced families like that of the Marquess of Salisbury.

Everything therefore became far easier and considerably more pleasant for the aristocrats of the Prince's age, or those a little older.

But this did not make it any easier for the Marchioness of Claydon to accept that, to put it bluntly, the Earl of Sherburn was bored with her.

She had tried to delude herself into believing it was just a transitory mood and that he would return to her.

But the intervals between his visits became longer and longer, and his explanations that he had other pressing business to attend to were not convincing.

When it became clear that that 'business' was Lady Esme Meldrum, the Marchioness's anger and jealousy were almost uncontainable.

Never in her whole life had she hated anybody as much as she hated Lady Esme.

She would stare in the mirror for hours wondering why her beauty had failed to hold the Earl when, in the opinion of most people, with her dark hair, flashing eyes and distinguished features, she was far more attractive than her rival.

But at last she had to accept that the Earl had gone, and for the last month she had not seen him until they had met today with all the other guests at Alchester Castle.

It had given her a shock when he had come into the Salon before dinner, and to the Marchioness's considerable annoyance her heart had turned a somersault and she had found it hard to breathe.

She had been very severe with herself during the last few weeks.

Her pride had told her not to whine as so many other women had done when they had lost the Earl, and she had determined to pretend, even if nobody believed her, that she had been the first to bring their affair to an end, because he no longer amused her.

The Marchioness might have many faults, but she was not the type of woman to be crushed by adversity, or to weep and wail even if she had lost what mattered most to her in life.

She told herself she would fight and go on fighting,

and even if in the end she did not get the Earl back again, she would somehow make him sorry for the way he had treated her.

Sooner or later, she thought, she would take her revenge on Esme Meldrum also and make her suffer as she was suffering.

Perhaps way back in the Marchioness's antecedents there was an Italian or a Spanish ancestor who understood what was meant by a vendetta.

All of the Earl's other discarded women had wept helplessly, but had done nothing else.

The Marchioness was determined she would be different.

"I will punish him," she told her reflection in the mirror, "if it is the last thing I ever do."

She would lie awake at night thinking of the misfortunes and the disasters she would inflict upon the Earl, until one day he would crawl back to her on his hands and knees and beg for mercy.

It was a fantasy that for a few moments at any rate assuaged the pain of her loss which was like a physical wound in her heart.

Now as she watched him walk into the Salon and greet the Prince, she knew that no man had ever made her feel as he had when he kissed her.

She despised herself for knowing that if at this moment he held out his arms to her she would run towards him like a homing pigeon.

Instead, holding herself tightly erect, she said as he approached her:

"Good evening, Osmond! It is delightful to see you again."

"There is no need for me to tell you that you are more beautiful than ever!" the Earl replied lightly.

His voice sounded as if he was speaking sincerely, but the expression in his eyes told the Marchioness what she already knew, that he no longer had any interest in her, and she hated him anew.

With an effort, because it was difficult to find her voice she said:

"George is looking forward to seeing you, and let me introduce you to George's niece, poor Peter's daughter, who has just come to live with us."

She indicated as she spoke a girl standing by her side who was obviously very young and self-effacing.

"Forella," the Marchioness continued, "this is the Earl of Sherburn, who owns the finest race-horses in England, and is also renowned as a great sportsman."

The Marchioness made the description sound almost an insult, and the Earl, appreciating that she was being sarcastic, merely bowed to her niece and moved towards Lady Esme who was standing on the other side of the room.

The way she held out her hand and the expression in her eyes as she looked at him told the Marchioness all too clearly what she knew already.

There was murder in her heart as she turned with an exaggerated effusiveness to greet another of her fellow guests.

*   *   *   *   *

Standing beside her aunt, Forella wondered why she was so angry.

In the strange life she had lived with her father Forella had learnt not only to judge people by what they said and how they looked, but to feel the vibrations that came from them.

She was well aware as soon as she arrived a week ago at her uncle's house in Park Lane that her aunt was not at all pleased to see her.

She knew the Marchioness was resenting with every nerve in her body that since she had no other

16

home, she was to live with them.

Although Forella had not been actually present at the arguments which had ensued over what should be done about her, she was perceptively aware.

From the moment she arrived from Italy, where her father had died in Naples during an epidemic of typhoid, she knew that as far as her aunt was concerned she was unwelcome.

"Are you telling me, George," the Marchioness had asked incredulously, "that your brother's child, whom I have never even seen, is to live with us? And I must present her at Court and bring her out as a *débutante*?"

"There is nothing else we can do, Kathie," the Marquess had replied sharply. "Now that Peter is dead, I am the girl's guardian, and as she is nearly nineteen she should have made her *début* a year ago."

"That was not likely to happen while she was rampaging about the world with her eccentric father!" the Marchioness replied sharply.

"I am aware of that," the Marquess said, "but if Peter liked to lead his life his way, it was no business of ours. But now he is dead we have to do what is right and proper for his daughter."

"She must have other relations who would be only too glad to take care of her if you paid them enough money to do so?"

"They are not in the same position as we are," the Marquess replied, "and I consider her my responsibility until she marries."

There was silence. Then the Marchioness exclaimed:

"What you are really saying is that I have to find her a husband!"

"Why not?" the Marquess enquired. "You have plenty of eligible nincompoops hanging about the place, drinking my wine and availing themselves of my hospitality. Surely one of them would be suitable to marry my niece?"

"With no dowry?" the Marchioness asked scathingly. "And I imagine after the life she has led with your brother, very few social graces!"

"She is an exceedingly pretty girl," the Marquis replied, "and I suppose you can smarten her up and teach her what she needs to know."

His wife did not reply and after a moment he said in a more conciliatory tone:

"Come on, Kathie, you were young yourself not so long ago, and we can hardly leave the girl sitting in some slum in Naples with nobody to look after her except for Peter's servant, who travelled with him all through the years."

"You are not expecting to bring him here as well?" the Marchioness enquired.

"No, I intend to pension him off," the Marquess replied. "He is a good man, and the least I can do is to give him a cottage in the country."

There was silence for a moment. Then the Marchioness said:

"And the girl?"

"She will be arriving in three weeks' time. I have arranged for a nun and a courier to bring her across France. I thought it only right that she should have time to get over her father's death."

The word death seemed to offer a speck of light to the Marchioness, in the darkness of what her husband was asking her to do.

"If Forella is in mourning she can hardly expect to attend Balls, and nobody wants a little black crow at any party."

"That is something that need not trouble you," the Marquess replied.

"Why not?" his wife enquired.

"Because Peter who, as you know, was always unconventional, left a note in his will to the effect that nobody was to mourn for him, nobody was to wear black, and he wished to be buried quietly without any fuss."

The Marquess paused. Then he added:

"My brother wrote to me:

I have had a damned good life, and have enjoyed every moment of it. If anybody misses me then I hope they will drink a glass of champagne to my memory and wish me luck, wherever I may be in the future."

There was a little break in the Marquess's voice as he repeated what his brother had said, but the Marchioness merely snorted:

"That sounds exactly the sort of nonsense your brother would write," she said, "but I suppose it makes it easier for me to do what you wish about his child. At the same time, George, do not think it will be easy for me, because it will not!"

"What you are saying," the Marquess replied, "is that you very much dislike the idea of having to chaperon a débutante. Because I am not a fool I appreciate that, Kathie. So the best thing you can do is to get her married off quickly. Then she will be off your hands and mine."

He paused before he added:

"I will give her three hundred a year which should make it easier, and you can spend what you like in decking her out."

For the first time since he began talking to her the Marchioness's eyes were less stormy.

"That is unusually generous of you, George!"

"I was fond of Peter," the Marquess said reflectively, "and although you may not believe it, I often envied him."

He did not say any more but went from the room while the Marchioness stared after him in astonishment.

How could George who had everything, a famous title, great wealth and a position both at Court and in Society, envy his brother?

She had not seen Peter Claye very often, but when she did she found him incomprehensible and, if she was honest, because she did not understand him, she disliked him.

Peter had actually been the third son of the previous Marquess and he therefore had not the slightest chance of succeeding to the title.

By the time George had married and had a son, Peter had begun to live a very different life from the rest of his family.

It was, of course, traditional that the youngest sons should have very little, while all the money and possessions were entailed onto the heir.

He had, therefore, knowing he could not live the social life which entertained and amused his two brothers, set off on his own to explore the world.

He had soon spent his small amount of capital and had to rely on the allowance he received every six months from the family Solicitors.

It was enough to allow him to travel as he wished, to marry, and be exceedingly happy with a wife who enjoyed the same strange roving life that interested him.

Their only child, Forella, before she could walk had travelled over deserts on the back of a camel.

Later she was dragged up the sides of mountains, sailed in creaking ships across strange seas to places where an English man and woman were a rarity, and the natives either stared or threatened them.

Occasionally, when his wife compelled him, Peter

Claye would sit down and write of his journeys and the unusual things he had seen for the Royal Geographical Society.

But usually, while he talked about writing a book, he was too busy living his life to have the time to set it down on paper.

"I will do that when I am too old to put one foot in front of the other," he would say laughing.

Then they would go off again to some other place which Peter thought would be exciting, and which he therefore wished to visit.

To Forella it was all a kaleidoscope of colour, new people, strange customs, and she found them as absorbing as her father did.

Only when her mother died did she realise that he was now her responsibility and she must look after him as he was obviously quite incapable of looking after her.

Never in his life had Peter Claye ever been able to worry about tomorrow.

His whole philosophy had been: 'Enjoy today, for tomorrow may never come.'

It came to him when, desperately short of money, they had lodged in what were really the slums of Naples while he decided where they would go next.

They had been warned there were a number of cases of typhoid in the City, but he had laughed.

"It may be dangerous, Papa," Forella had said.

"I am indestructible!" he boasted, and a week later he died.

It was Jackson, Peter's servant, who had had the sense to write to the Marquess.

When he told Forella what he had done she was angry with him.

"Why did you do that?" she asked. "Uncle George has paid no attention to us for years. Why should he worry about me now?"

"He has to worry about you, Miss Forella," Jackson answered.

"Why?"

"Because now that your father's dead, God rest his soul, His Lordship's your Guardian, and he's got to do something about you."

Forella had looked at the wiry little man with troubled eyes.

"What do you mean by that? I do not want anybody to look after me."

"Now look 'ere, Miss Forella," Jackson said, "now the Master's no longer with us, we've got to do what's right and proper and what your mother, lovely lady that she were, would have wanted, if she were alive."

"I do not know what you are saying," Forella said.

But she had known, and it terrified her.

Sure enough, two weeks later, the Marquess had arrived in Naples in answer to Jackson's letter.

Because he resembled her father in looks and was extremely kind and unexpectedly understanding, Forella had cried for the first time since her father had died.

"I miss him, Uncle George,' she said. "He was such fun to be with, and nothing will ever be the same again."

"I know, my dear," the Marquess replied, "but now you have to live a new sort of life, and that means coming to England with me."

"Oh, no!" Forella exclaimed involuntarily.

"You do not like the idea?"

"It . . . it frightens me," Forella explained. "Papa used to laugh and tell me how smart and important you and Aunt Kathie were."

She paused, before she went on:

"Sometimes we would read about you in a newspaper, which was usually weeks old, when we were in Singapore, or Hong Kong, or somewhere like that, and Papa would say:

" 'There you are, Forella, my brother George is lording it above them all, and I am proud of him, very proud. But thank God, I do not have to live his life, even if he is "Monarch of all he surveys"!' "

The Marquis laughed.

"I can hear Peter say that. He always thought Society was a joke."

There was silence. Then Forella had said in a very small voice:

"Please, Uncle George . . . could I not . . . stay here with . . . Jackson?"

The Marquess had taken her hand in his.

"Now listen to me, Forella," he said. "Jackson is a very nice little man, but he is getting on in years, while you are young, very young, and you have all your life in front of you."

His fingers tightened comfortingly as he went on:

"Now you have to become a lady in the full sense of the word. That is what is best for you and what I believe in his heart your father would have wanted where you were concerned."

Because Forella had the uneasy feeling that this was true, she could not find words in which to go on arguing.

Although she tried to forget it, she could remember her mother saying when they were in some obscure and rather uncomfortable part of the world:

"When Forella is eighteen, we shall have to go back to England, darling, and give her a chance to enjoy all the things which you have given up, and which I never wanted."

Listening, Forella had been quite certain her father would say it was an absurd idea, but in fact, he had

23

replied:

"Can you really see us all dolled up at Buckingham Palace with Forella wearing those ridiculous white feathers on her head and trying to curtsy without tripping up over her train?"

"Yes, I can!" his wife said firmly.

There had been a little pause. Then her father had said:

"Anyway, if I have to suffer that discomfort, which will be far worse than anything we have found here, I shall at least be escorting the two most beautiful women ever to enter the Throne Room!"

Forella had never thought of that conversation again.

But now because since he had died everything her father had said to her seemed to come vividly to her mind, she had not argued any further with the Marquess.

He had therefore made arrangements for her and Jackson to be escorted to London, as soon as they were clear of the quarantine which had been imposed on Naples since the epidemic of typhoid.

Three weeks later she had arrived at Park Lane and had known the moment she saw her aunt that she was unwanted and unwelcome.

Nevertheless, the Marchioness had done what was expected of her and, although Forella was not aware of it, she had taken to heart her husband's suggestion that the girl should be married as quickly as possible.

She had taken Forella to the best shops and provided her with gowns she had never thought it possible she would own.

Her hair had been cut and shaped by the most important and expensive *coiffeur* in London, and everything she had brought with her from Italy had been either thrown away or burnt.

'I am no longer myself,' Forella thought a dozen times, 'but a puppet with Aunt Kathie pulling the strings and making very certain that I do not think for myself, let alone say anything that has not been approved by her first.'

Because her education had been extremely cosmopolitan, she had learnt a dozen languages in different parts of the world, could calculate in the same number of currencies and cook better than most chefs.

Now her aunt concentrated on having Forella taught to dance, and a teacher of deportment had come every day to teach her how to walk into a room, use a fan, to bow, to curtsy and to shake hands.

She learnt to sit so that she did not show her ankle, and as little as possible of the toe of her shoe.

Actually she had learnt many of the dances of the East in order to amuse her father. She had watched the dance of the Seven Veils and without understanding what they were portraying, the exotic dance of the Ouled Nails.

Her teacher had therefore found her a very quick pupil, with a grace and suppleness that was different from the rather stiff, often gauche débutantes he had taught before.

Deportment had been just as easy.

"Shall I show you how the Japanese greet their visitors?" Forella had asked. "And this is how the South Sea Islanders do it."

When this made him recoil in horror, she had laughed at the expression on his face until he laughed too, and the Marchioness had come into the room to demand why they were making so much noise.

By the time she was ready to attend her first Ball Forella felt that she had been transformed from a rough, uncut stone into a finished and polished gem, and just, she said to herself, 'as hard and uninteresting.'

When she was allowed to meet some of her aunt's friends she found the best thing she could do was to keep silent.

She soon realised they were not in the least interested in her – in fact, girls in her position were expected to be seen and not heard.

Her aunt's feelings had not changed in the slightest since she had come to live with them in Park Lane, so Forella kept out of her way as much as she could.

Her uncle was always unfailingly kind, and often when he returned home from the House of Lords she would slip into his Study, where he relaxed and read the newspapers, to talk to him.

To her surprise he was really interested in her father's travels.

He would ask her to tell him the whole story of her father's attempt to find the source of the Nile, and explain to him how they had got on with the various tribes in the Sudan who were supposed to be hostile.

"Once or twice," Forella said with a smile, "Mama would think our last hour had come. But Papa was so clever with those people, and of course he could speak their language, which made all the difference."

"I wonder where he got that gift?" the Marquess asked thoughtfully. "I was never very good myself, even at French. Those 'Frogs' talk too fast for me to understand a word they say!"

Forella laughed.

"Papa could make himself understood anywhere, and Mama found every language easy after her own."

"Of course," the Marquess agreed, "but then she was a foreigner."

He did not mean to say it unkindly, but merely as if it was somewhat of a disadvantage.

Her aunt had actually made it quite clear that her mother's nationality should be forgotten if Forella was to be a success in the Social World.

"Foreigners, unless they are French or Royal, are really not very acceptable," she said in a lofty tone. "Of course, Kings and Princes are a different thing altogether. At the same time, we have to find you an English husband and forget that most unfortunately you are not yourself wholly English."

There was obviously no point in arguing, so Forella had merely said meekly:

"Yes, Aunt Kathie."

"It will be no use being too particular," the Marchioness had gone on. "You have, as your uncle's niece, that one great asset, but unfortunately not much money. Anyway, we will make the very best of the fact that you are a Claye, and nobody can deny they are one of the most aristocratic families in the country."

Forella tried to forget how her father laughed at snobs and those who climbed the social tree, and again because an answer was expected of her she merely said:

"Yes, Aunt Kathie."

She said 'yes' and 'no' to her partners at dinner when they spoke to her, who obviously found it was a bore to have a young girl next to them.

They were usually soon engrossed in flirting with the very much more sophisticated women on their other side.

It was, although Forella did not realise it, a great surprise for most of the people to find such a young girl at any party given by Prince János.

He had made it a rule for a long time that his parties should consist of his own very special friends who were more or less of the same age as he was.

The women might be slightly younger, but they were invariably married, and therefore as everybody had the same interests, the same jokes, and moved in the same circles there was no one to bore them or to make it a duty to be polite.

The only exception at the Prince's parties was usually an older woman who played hostess and took the place of his wiife.

The Prince's wife was a mystery, and he never spoke of her.

It was, however, generally assumed that she preferred to live in Hungary, although one or two people who had been to that country and had made enquiries could learn nothing about her.

As usual an older woman, on this occasion the scintillating and witty Lady Roehampton, played the part of hostess.

She was universally popular, and understood all the intrigues, the likes and dislikes of a party, which was expected in a really successful hostess.

In fact, Lady Roehampton had exclaimed in horror when the Prince told her that the Marquess had asked if he and his wife could bring his niece for the weekend.

"A young girl? My dear János, you must be crazy! She will be a fish out of water!"

"I realise that," the Prince replied, "but I found it impossible to refuse Claydon. After all, if you remember it was George who proposed me for White's Club when I first came to England, and also sponsored me when I wished to join the Jockey Club."

He smiled at his success since then and finished:

"I have always felt that I owe him a debt of gratitude, and this is one way I can repay it."

"I understand all that," Lady Roehampton replied. "At the same time, a young girl! Oh dear! What shall I do with her?"

"As I gather from George she has just arrived from abroad and knows nothing of England, I should just forget her."

The Prince laughed before he added:

"If you ask me, she will just watch everything wide-eyed and find the whole thing entirely incomprehensible, as I am sure you would have done at that age."

"It is too long ago for me to remember!" Lady Roehampton replied.

She put her hand on his arm.

"You are quite right, János, you could not have refused George. But I am prepared to wager that Kathie is furious at having to take a young girl about with her."

"In which case I am sorry for the child," the Prince remarked.

"I suppose you realise," Lady Roehampton went on, "that Kathie has lost Osmond?"

The Prince started.

"Are you telling me their affair is over?"

"Of course it is, about three weeks ago, after you went to Paris. Now I hear, although I may be wrong, that Osmond is now *epris* with Esme Meldrum."

"Good Heavens!" the Prince exclaimed. "And they are all coming here this weekend. You should have told me before."

Lady Roehampton spread out her hands in an expressive gesture.

"Why worry? They all have to meet sooner or later, and besides it will give everybody else a great deal to talk about!"

The Prince sighed.

"I hope you are right, but I have a good mind to ask Esme Meldrum and Richard to come another time."

"I think they would consider that an extremely rude thing to do," Lady Roehampton said. "Besides, I am not sure I am right in thinking there is something between Esme and Richard."

She wrinkled her brow and continued:

"It is just a whisper at the moment, yet I suppose it was inevitable that Esme would attract Osmond's roving eye and he would find that pink-and-white Dresden china look of hers irresistible."

"Of course – irresistible!" the Prince agreed.

Lady Roehampton looked at him sharply.

"Do you mean . . . are you telling me, János . . .?"

"No, no!" the Prince replied. "That would complicate things even more than they are already."

There was a smile on his face as he walked away, and looking after him Lady Roehampton wondered if any woman would ever capture the heart of János Kovác.

Knowing him as well as she did, she still found him an enigma, still unpredictable, still a man, she thought in her old age, more attractive and intriguing than any man she had ever met in her long life.

However, she did not pretend to understand him, and she had the strange feeling as she thought about him that he did not understand himself.

2

As soon as the gentlemen joined the ladies the Earl, without making too much effort to be discreet, gravitated towards Esme Meldrum.

He thought as she stood against a background of exotic flowers, apparently looking out at the last rays of the setting sun, that she was very beautiful.

The Prince, unlike most hosts, would never have the curtains drawn until night had actually fallen.

The candles were lit in the chandeliers in the Salon and glittered on the diamonds around Esme's neck. But they were not as brilliant, the Earl thought, as the light in her eyes.

He was aware, being very experienced with women, that it was because she was looking at him that she appeared so radiant, and there was also an undeniable invitation in the soft smile on her lips.

For a moment he stood looking at her without speaking. Then when she appeared to question his silence, he said:

"I think we both know that while you are watching the sunset, for us it is the prelude to dawn."

"Are you sure that is what you . . . want it to be?" she enquired.

"As that is quite an unnecessary question, I shall answer it later," he said.

There was a little pause before he asked:

"In which room are you sleeping?"

She gave him a glance which told him that just as he desired her she felt the same, and he thought it was a gift from the gods that Richard Meldrum was not arriving until tomorrow.

Quickly, before she could reply, he said:

"I think as this place is large enough to house a Regiment we had better follow the example set by the Prince of Wales."

Esme laughed and he laughed too.

They were both aware that when the Prince made advances to a pretty girl in a house with which he was not familiar, he always suggested that she should identify her bedroom for him by placing a rose outside the door.

"Perhaps that would be wise," Esme agreed. "After all, although I think I am on the same floor as you, there are a great number of bedrooms and I would not like you to get lost."

The way she spoke told the Earl all he wished to know, and he thought it would be wise now to move away from her. He could join several other men who were discussing where they should play cards or gratify a dozen of the other ladies by his attention.

But spoilt because he always got his own way, he decided there was only one person he wanted to talk to at this moment and stayed where he was.

Prince János, having indicated to his other guests that card tables were waiting for them in an adjoining room, looked round to see if he had left anyone out and saw the Marchioness of Claydon shimmering in green sequins, standing by the fireplace.

As he started to walk towards her he realised she was not watching his approach, but looking at two people talking together by the window.

The expression on her face and the anger in her eyes were so vivid that the Prince did not have to guess who was upsetting her.

Instead with the tact for which he was famous and the charm which was irresistible he went up to her and taking her hand in his, said:

"I do not have to tell you, Kathie, that you are the most beautiful woman here tonight, and every time I see you I am convinced you grow lovelier."

For a moment the Marchioness's eyes widened with surprise.

The Prince had always been courteous and delightful to her, and she was extremely gratified that she and George were so often included in his parties.

He had, however, never singled her out, and because he was so unpredictable she had never considered even for a moment that he might become her lover.

She would of course have been thrilled if there were the slightest chance of it, for to capture the heart of the Prince János Kovác would have been a feather in any woman's cap. But she had never given even a fleeting thought to anything so wildly improbable.

Now for the first time it flashed through her mind that if he really found her attractive he would certainly be a very adequate replacement for the Earl.

Half shutting her eyes and looking at him in the enigmatic manner which she had found in the past intrigued any man, she replied:

"Dear János, you are always so kind, and I wish I could believe that you are speaking truthfully."

"How can you doubt it?" the Prince asked. "And Kathie, I have just bought a picture about which I should like your opinion. I think it will amuse you because there is a certain resemblance in it to yourself."

Without waiting for the Marchioness to reply, he drew her from the Salon and took her across the Hall into a very attractive Sitting-Room in which the picture to which he was referring had been hung over the mantelpiece.

It was a portrait of an unknown Venetian woman painted in the early 18th century.

She was not only very beautiful, but there was undoubtedly, the Marchioness could see, in the dark hair and the dark eyes of the sitter, a faint resemblance to herself.

She was aware as she looked up arching her neck to show what had often been called 'the exquisite outline of it', that the Prince was watching her.

Then she said very softly:

"Thank you, János. At the same time, you flatter me."

"How can I do that?" the Prince asked, "when you are well aware that you are the Belle of every Ball you attend? I noticed there was no one to touch you at Marlborough House the other night, and I heard Prince Albert say the same thing."

"Shall I pretend that you are making me feel shy?" the Marchioness enquired. "Or shall I ask you to tell me more?"

"It is something I am only too willing to do," the Prince replied, "but as you well know, I must first look after my guests. All the same, Kathie, we have the whole weekend in front of us."

As he spoke he took her hand in his and turned it over and kissed the palm.

It was a very graceful gesture and one at which the Prince was extremely proficient.

It made the Marchioness draw in her breath, and as they walked hand in hand towards the door she was

34

smiling, and looking very different from the way she had in the Salon.

The Prince escorted her to the Card-Room and sitting down at the Baccarat table where a number of the other guests were waiting for him to take the Bank, he put the Marchioness on his right saying as he did so:

"I feel you will bring me luck and tonight we will play together."

The Marchioness was delighted. For she knew this meant that he would cover her losses, while any games that ensued would be hers.

However rich anybody was in the Social World, they were never too rich to refuse more.

The Marchioness was already thinking as they started to play that she might after all be able to buy a sable stole she wanted but which George had refused to give her on the grounds that it was too expensive.

Because the Prince was so rich and the majority of his guests were also very wealthy, the stakes at the Baccarat table were very high.

As a perfect host, Prince János usually contrived that those who could not afford to lose found themselves without realising what was happening seated at a Bridge-table.

It was two hours later before the Marchioness's thoughts returned to the Earl and Esme Meldrum.

By that time the pile of gold coins in front of her at the Baccarat table had pleasingly multiplied.

Only as she lost at the last turn of the cards did she think perhaps her luck had changed, and she would be wise to move while she was still a large winner.

As if the Prince realised what she was thinking, he said:

"I am sure you would like a glass of champagne. Shall we go and find one before I start a new shoe?"

"That would be delightful!" the Marchioness replied.

They rose from the table and one of the guests asked quickly:

"You are not leaving, Kovác?"

"No, of course not," the Prince replied. "Just stretching our legs and looking for something with which to quench our thirst."

"You might be allowed to drink a toast to yourself," came the reply, "but hurry back, I am determined to have my revenge."

"You shall have it," the Prince replied good-humouredly.

He walked with the Marchioness into the Salon next door and was aware as he did so that at the far end of it seated on a sofa were the Earl and Esme Meldrum, talking to each other intimately.

There were two other people in the room, and the Marchioness saw with surprise that it was her husband with Forella beside him.

They too were talking, but animatedly, and as she and the Prince walked towards them Forella's laughter rang out spontaneously.

Because she looked so lovely, and at the same time the Marchioness was acutely aware of how interested the Earl was in her rival, she had to find fault with somebody.

She therefore stopped beside her husband and said to Forella:

"I hoped by this time you would have had the sense to go to bed, and not bother your poor uncle, who I am sure is longing to be at the card table where he usually is!"

"That is just where you are mistaken!" the Marquess replied, before his niece could speak. "Forella and I have been having an extremely interesting talk and I am enjoying myself."

"I am glad to hear it," the Marchioness said, obviously not really attending to what he was saying but looking out of the corner of her eye at the Earl on the other side of the room.

The Prince came from the side table where he had poured out two glasses of champagne. As he handed one to her, he asked:

"What about you, George? Shall I get you a drink?"

"Do not worry," the Marquess replied. "I will get one for myself. As a matter of fact, your wines at dinner were so excellent that I am not thirsty."

"I hoped you would enjoy them."

It was then the Marchioness realised that Forella was standing at her uncle's side waiting to say goodnight, but she deliberately turned her back to talk to the Prince.

Even so, she could hear Forella say:

"Thank you, Uncle George, you have been so kind, and I have enjoyed this evening more than I can tell you."

She kissed his cheek, then obviously wishing to escape from her aunt's condemnation moved quickly across the room towards the door.

The Marchioness thought as she did so that the sooner she could get the girl married the better.

It was then, almost as it were out of the blue, that an idea came to her.

*　　*　　*　　*　　*

Once in the Hall Forella did not hurry, but walked slowly up the magnificent carved staircase, thinking that the Castle was the finest building she had ever seen and certainly the grandest at which she had ever stayed.

She told herself that whatever anybody else did

tomorrow she would find somebody to show her round and especially the pictures.

It was her mother who had been interested in art and had made her visit the Museums whenever they were in a city that had one.

She had also taught her to appreciate the beauties of the strange lands they visited.

"There is beauty everywhere, darling," she had said once, "and you do not have to own beauty to capture it, for you can hold it in your mind so that whether you are rich or poor it is yours for ever afterwards."

It was something Forella had always remembered.

Now walking along a corridor with its magnificent pieces of furniture, huge carved mirrors and pictures by old masters, she told herself that it was all hers.

'The next time I am sleeping in a tent in the desert,' she thought, 'or in a confined cabin of some small smelly steam-ship I will conjure up what I am seeing now.'

Then she remembered with a pang in her heart that there would be no more voyages into the unknown, no more hardships and adventures which were always exciting in retrospect.

Instead there would be just the social life she was experiencing with her aunt and uncle and which she found at times dull and at others incomprehensible.

'They eat and talk, talk and eat, and that goes on day after day,' she thought. 'No wonder the men grow fat and the women catty!'

Because she was extremely intelligent, although she was ignorant of the Social World, she had not missed the spiteful things her aunt often said about other women to her friends, to her husband, and when there was no one else there, to Forella herself.

She had also discovered that her aunt had a very

different voice for the handsome, good-looking men who when visiting the house did not pay her special attention, but were obviously a very close and intimate part of her aunt's daily existence.

Forella did not understand their jokes, and all their innuendos went over her head.

At the same time, she knew it was all very paltry and unimportant, and she longed to be talking to her father about the customs of the Berbers, and significance of Mecca to a Moslem, or planning with him an expedition which would take them into territory where few other Europeans had ever ventured.

"Oh, Papa," she cried out in her heart, "why did you have to leave me?"

She realised as the question seemed to vibrate on the air that she had reached her bedroom and a maid was waiting to help her undress.

This was a luxury she was not accorded in her uncle's house in Park Lane and she said quickly:

"I am sorry. I should have told you not to wait up for me."

"It's my duty, miss," the maid replied.

"Do you not get very tired?" Forella asked curiously.

"I sometimes get the chance, miss, of a lie down in the afternoon, and it's only at weekends when the house is full that we have to keep going for so long."

She did not wait for Forella to answer but went on:

"You're early, miss. I don't suppose the rest of the party'll come up until the early hours!"

Forella thought it was rather cruel especially for her aunt's maid, who she realised now would be waiting next door and was getting on in years.

Then she told herself it was not for her to criticise.

As her maid hung up her gown in the wardrobe she walked across the room to the communicating door to be quite certain it was tightly shut.

She thought as she did so with a little smile that if there was the slightest excuse for Aunt Kathie to complain she had kept her awake by snoring or by moving about the room she would not hesitate to find fault and to scold her in the morning.

The room in which Forella was sleeping was very large, and the huge bed draped with silk curtains was very impressive.

"I see you are next to your uncle and me," the Marchioness had said when they arrived, "and I think it is very considerate of Lady Roehampton. Young girls are usually in single rooms in another part of the Castle."

The way she spoke made Forella feel it was not so much a matter of congratulation as a reproof.

The Marchioness had made it very clear that it was very unusual for a young girl to be staying in any house-party which consisted of older people like herself.

"Where Prince János is concerned," she had added, "it is unheard of for anybody he entertains to be so young."

Forella could not think of a reply, so she remained silent.

"I hope you realise how fortunate you are," her aunt finished in the hard voice in which she habitually addressed her.

"I am very grateful, Aunt Kathie."

"And so you should be! At least you will be able to hold your own, as far as concerns your clothes. Heaven knows what your uncle will say when he sees the bills!"

Forella had heard this remark so often before that it had ceased to impress her as it had done at first.

She had actually said to the Marquess when they

40

were alone:

"Thank you, Uncle George, for being so kind and generous in giving me so many beautiful gowns, but I am sure I could do with fewer."

Her uncle had smiled and patted her shoulder.

"You are very pretty, my dear, and clothes are important to a woman."

"I know they are, but they are also very expensive!"

"You will not bankrupt me!" he smiled. "And when, as I undoubtedly will, I take you up the aisle to be married to somebody important, it will give me great pleasure."

Forella knew that by 'important' he meant somebody in the same society in which they moved themselves.

She longed to reply that she would much rather marry an explorer or a foreigner, and knew how horrified her aunt would be.

Ever since she reached London she had had it drummed into her day after day by her aunt that her father's way of life had been eccentric to the point of being outrageous, and that she was extremely fortunate to have been saved from it.

It was impossible to protest in reply that she would lie awake at night hating the softness of her bed, disliking the feeling of being confined between four walls, and longing instead for the wide-open spaces under a star-studded sky.

She yearned too for the turbulent waves of a strange sea moving beneath her.

'Aunt Kathie would never understand,' she thought despairingly, and knew there was no point in trying to tell anybody what she felt.

Now she drew back the heavy brocade curtains, pulled up the dark blinds and, opening all the windows, let in the night air.

It felt cool and refreshing after the heat of the rooms downstairs and Forella leaned out.

There were stars overhead but they were not as brilliant or as numerous as those which had shone over her in the East.

But there was enough light from the moon coming up the sky to see its reflection on the lake which lay in front of the house, and to be able to discern the ancient oak trees in the Park on the far side of it.

"If Papa were here," she told herself, "he would help me to study the history of the Castle, and to appreciate its treasures. At the same time he would laugh at the people who are staying in it, and refuse to take them seriously."

She told herself she must do the same, and that she had been feeling depressed because she was taking her new life with her uncle and aunt more seriously than was necessary.

"It is just an uncomfortable phase in my life," she told herself, "like climbing a mountain with a blistered foot, or sleeping in some of those little dak bungalows in India which had snakes in the rafters."

She could remember a time in Turkey when she and her father and mother had been caught in a terrible storm and had to shelter in a cave which smelt strongly of wild animals.

After they had been there for a short time they all began to itch from the bites of insects the animals had left behind them.

She remembered her father had sworn vigorously as he scratched himself, and when her mother had rebuked him laughingly, he had said:

"A few good British swear words never hurt anyone. I only hope the damned fleas understand English!"

They had all laughed and after that it had seemed a

tremendous joke.

"I have to laugh at everything that is happening to me," Forella told herself.

She got into bed to lie looking at the stars until she fell asleep.

*　　*　　*　　*　　*

Forella was dreaming that she was with her father when she was awoken by the sound of the door opening.

Because she had so often slept in very strange places she was a very light sleeper and had learned to wake to the rustle of a cobra slithering over the floor, or the snorting of a wild animal outside.

Then she was aware to her surprise that there was somebody just inside the door.

She could not see who it was because the light that came through her windows from the moon and stars did not penetrate that far.

Though she was aware there was somebody there, being still half asleep she was not for the moment afraid.

Then as the tall figure of a man began to cross the room towards the bed, she gave a little gasp and tried to ask:

"Who are . . . you? What do you . . . want?"

He said distinctly in a low voice:

"Esme?"

It was then as she opened her mouth to scream that the door of the communicating room opened and her aunt came into the room carrying a silver candelabra with lighted candles.

She was wearing an elaborate negligée of satin and lace and looked, Forella thought, most imposing and undeniably beautiful.

She was, however, not looking at her, but at the

43

man standing beside the bed with his back to the window.

Now Forella saw that it was the Earl of Sherburn who had frightened her.

As she looked at him she was aware that he was staring at her in utter astonishment and at the same time he seemed to be turned to stone.

The Marchioness's eyes met his across the room. Then she said in a clear tone which seemed to ring out in the silence:

"Really, Osmond, how can you do anything so outrageous as to attempt to seduce somebody as young as Forella?"

For a moment it seemed as if the Earl found it impossible to speak. Then at last he said:

"I am of course in the wrong room!"

"You can hardly expect me to believe that!" the Marchioness replied.

She spoke mockingly and there was, Forella thought, an unpleasant smile as it were of triumph on her lips.

She turned her head to call out:

"George, will you come here immediately? I told you there was somebody in Forella's bedroom."

As if her words galvanised the Earl into action he walked away from the side of the bed to the centre of the room to confront the Marchioness.

Although he spoke in a lowered voice it was possible for Forella to hear what he said.

"You are well aware, Kathie, of the truth of the matter, and it would be a great mistake for you to make a scene!"

"I am aware of nothing of the sort!" the Marchioness replied.

She had answered him in the same lowered voice that he had used.

Then as if without turning round she sensed that her husband had come into the room and was standing just behind her, she said:

"I can imagine nothing more disgraceful than that I should find you here!"

"What is all this about? What is going on?" the Marquess demanded.

"You may well ask, George," his wife replied. "I heard a sound, as I told you! So I came to investigate, and found Osmond at Forella's bedside!"

The Marquess for the moment seemed stunned.

"What is all this about, Sherburn?" he demanded. "You never met the girl until this evening!"

The Marchioness gave a very unpleasant laugh.

"For all we know, George, they may have been meeting each other in London, or else Osmond suddenly has developed a *penchant* for cradle-snatching. Anyway, the point is, what are you going to do about it?"

"What do you mean?" the Marquess asked.

"Then as if he was suddenly aware that something more was expected of him, he said:

"I suppose, Sherburn, you should apologise."

"I have already explained," the Earl replied, "that I made a mistake in coming into the wrong room. I expect you to believe me, George, even if your wife does not!"

"Well, of course, if . . . " the Marquess began, but the Marchioness interrupted him.

"My dear George, you must be aware that in the circumstances the only thing our good friend the Earl of Sherburn can do is to behave honourably. You cannot allow your niece's reputation to be dragged in the mud without his making the obvious reparation."

"Good God, you cannot mean . . .?" the Marquess asked.

"I mean," the Marchioness said decisively, "that the very least Osmond can do in the circumstances is to offer Forella marriage!"

There was a silence when she had spoken and the Earl held his breath.

Then Forella who had sat up in bed without being aware of it cried:

"No, no! Of course . . . not! It was a . . . mistake, Aunt Kathie. Of course it was a . . . mistake!"

She remembered as she spoke that she had seen the Earl talking to the beautiful Lady Meldrum on the sofa, and had thought vaguely while she was chatting to her uncle how attractive they looked together.

It was almost, she told herself, as if they were the hero and heroine in a play.

She was aware, although she could not hear what they said, that the Earl was flirting with Lady Esme, and she was flirting with him with her eyes, her lips and the little gestures she made with her hands.

It was so fascinating that Forella had wanted to watch them, but knew it would be embarrassing if they realised she was staring at them.

She had therefore forced herself not to look more than she could help in their direction, but to keep her eyes on her uncle.

Now, of course, she understood that the Earl had wanted to be alone with Lady Esme, which he could not be downstairs.

He had therefore intended to go to her bedroom and doubtless she had been expecting him, but by mistake he had come into hers.

As she spoke the Marchioness turned to her with an unmistakable expression of anger in her eyes, as she said:

"You be quiet! Doubtless you are as much to blame for this immoral behaviour as he is! Let me point out,

Forella, that no man would have come to your bedroom unless you had encouraged him!"

Her aunt's attack was so astonishing that for a moment Forella could only stare at her open-mouthed.

Then as she tried to find words in which to express her own innocence the Marquess said:

"I suppose, Sherburn, the only thing you can do in the circumstances is to make the best of it. After all, I cannot have my niece's reputation soiled by scandal at her age."

Again there was silence and Forella, looking apprehensively at the Earl, thought she had never seen a man look so grim and at the same time so contemptuous.

He was not looking at her uncle, but at her aunt as he said:

"Very well, you win! I will marry your niece, and I hope she enjoys being my wife!"

His words seemed to vibrate round the room.

Then as he finished speaking he walked to the door, pulled it open and as he went out slammed it behind him.

Forella found her voice again.

"No . . . please . . . Uncle George. It is all a . . . terrible mistake . . .!" she began.

"I daresay that is the truth," the Marquess interrupted, "but your aunt is right. You cannot afford to have your reputation smeared before you have even been presented."

As he finished speaking he walked through the communicating door into his own bedroom, and Forella watched him go with a feeling of despair.

"Wait . . . please wait . . . Uncle George . . . !" she cried.

The Marchioness walked to the foot of the bed to

say:

"Shut up, and do not be such a little fool! I have got you a husband that most girls would go on their knees to marry, and although he will doubtless lead you a hell of a life, you will be the Countess of Sherburn!"

She seemed almost to spit the words at Forella. Then as if she could not bear the sight of her she turned away abruptly and followed her husband taking the candelabra with her.

Forella gave a little cry of sheer horror.

She could hardly believe it had all happened and felt she must still be dreaming and this was a nightmare.

Then she knew that it was impossible, completely and absolutely impossible, for her to be married to a man she did not know and had only met for one brief second, and who she was well aware was in love with somebody else.

"I cannot do it! Oh, Papa, save me!" she prayed.

Getting out of bed she walked to the window to stand looking at the stars.

*　　*　　*　　*　　*

Having reached his own bedroom the Earl was feeling very much the same as Forella, as if he had stepped into a nightmare from which he could not extricate himself.

He understood only too well what had happened: after everyone had gone to bed, Kathie must have looked to see if there was a rose outside Esme's bedroom.

Looking back now into the past he remembered on one occasion how they had laughed together about the Prince's arrangement with a woman who had taken his fancy.

It was obvious therefore that Kathie had guessed

48

that he would use that means tonight of identifying Esme's bedroom.

It was a revenge, he told himself, that was too severe for the crime.

After all, no *affaire de coeur* in which he was involved lasted very long, and it was unusual for the women he left, generally in tears, to become an enemy.

He always tried to make them into friends in the same way as the Prince of Wales managed to do.

It was well known that when one of his love affairs ended he was invariably loyal to the lady in question, as she was loyal to him.

But where the Earl was concerned there had been unfortunate moments in the past when the lady in whom he was no longer interested had made a scene and had threatened him.

But never had any such threat, however dramatic, been put into operation.

Now he thought the Marchioness had succeeded where the others had failed, and for the moment he could not think how he could extricate himself from a situation which was not only intolerable, but also exceedingly humiliating.

He had no wish, at least not for many years, to marry anybody – least of all, he thought savagely, a very young girl who might make him a submissive wife, but with whom he would be bored stiff within a month of their marriage.

What was more, every instinct in him resented being pressurised into marriage or, to put it bluntly, caught as he had been.

"I will not do it! I am damned if I will!" he told himself.

But as he flung himself down on his bed he thought it might as well be a bed of nails and he could not imagine what he could do to escape.

The Marchioness held every trump-card and had certainly played them.

In the meantime he was aware that if he was to take any action to free himself he would have to act quickly.

He was sure that Kathie would tomorrow inform Lady Roehampton, if not the Prince, that he had proposed to Forella.

For the girl's sake she would not specify in what circumstances. But, if he knew the way her brain worked, she would probably insinuate that they had been meeting in London ever since Forella had arrived from Naples.

She would then say that he had seized the opportunity last night when they were all at the Castle to inform her aunt and uncle of his intentions.

There would be doubts concerning the truth of this in the minds of quite a number of people who had observed his behaviour with Esme Meldrum.

They would, however, be delighted that having been elusive for so long he had been caught in the bonds of matrimony – bonds being definitely the right word for it.

He could almost hear their gushing congratulations and their cynical good wishes for his future happiness.

"What the devil can I do?" he asked himself aloud in the darkness.

It flashed through his mind that he might go abroad, but that would solve nothing for he could not stay away indefinitely.

He knew without even thinking about it that to appeal to Forella was hopeless as she would inevitably be overruled by her aunt and uncle.

He did not even have to consider how delighted

Kathie would be not to have a young girl clinging round her.

The Earl was extremely knowledgeable in the psychology of women, and he had known immediately on hearing from some gossip-monger that George Claydon had a niece coming out this Season that Kathie would be furious.

"I hate young girls!" she had said to him once when they were together. "I cannot imagine how they ever turn into amusing and witty women!"

"You must have been very young yourself once!" he had said mockingly.

"Never!" Kathie had exclaimed. "I was born old and wise in everything that mattered and with a knowledge of witchcraft which you yourself have complained about."

"Of course," the Earl had agreed. "You bewitched me from the first moment I saw you."

It was the answer she wanted, and as her arms went round his neck and he felt her body moving against his, he had told himself she had an enchantment he found irresistible.

But witches could be dangerous, and he knew now he should never have become involved with Kathie in the first place.

He had always preferred fair women with blue eyes who were usually rather stupid.

While the Marchioness was undoubtedly one of the most beautiful women he had ever seen, her black hair and black eyes should have warned him that she could be deeply revengeful and implacably dangerous as he now knew to his cost.

But it was too late.

He had walked into the trap she had set for him, and no amount of struggling would get him out of it.

3

The Prince always awoke early in the morning and usually went out riding at about six o'clock.

This morning, however, when he opened his eyes and saw the sun streaming in through the open window it was an hour earlier.

He had gone to bed with a certain worry on his mind which was still there for his instinct, which because of his Hungarian blood was unusually perceptive, had told him that something was wrong.

He was not certain what it was except that he thought it concerned the Marchioness and Lady Esme.

But a red flag was being waved in front of him and nothing could stop him from feeling this strange and unaccountable apprehension.

Because whenever he woke he needed to be active, he got up and dressed himself without ringing for his valet, walked downstairs and out towards the stables.

By this time a few of the younger housemaids in their mob-caps and gingham dresses were beginning to pull back the curtains and clean out the grates.

There were also, the Prince was aware, footmen in their shirt-sleeves clearing away the glasses from where they had been left in the Salon and card room.

Later the older servants would be appearing to supervise them and give instructions to ensure that everything was in perfect order by the time he or his guests appeared.

The fact that he was unusually early caused the servants to give him quick questioning glances as if they felt something must be wrong.

But the Prince walked purposefully towards the stables, feeling that what he wanted more than anything else was to ride one of his most spirited horses.

He would then enjoy a battle for supremacy in which he was invariably the victor, but with the satisfaction of knowing he had had to fight for it.

He regularly brought over from Hungary horses that were only half trained and he knew that his experience with horseflesh was greatly admired not only by his friends but by everybody he employed.

He reached the stables which since he had bought the Castle had been completely rebuilt.

He always congratulated himself not only on the architect's skill in designing the building to match the architecture of the Castle, especially the Georgian part of it, but also that his horses were housed in greater comfort than those of any other owner in the country.

Because he was so early there was only a stable-boy on duty who gave him a startled glance, then hurried to alert the Head Groom.

The Prince moved down the long line of stalls deciding which horse he would ride and seeing with pleasure that one which had arrived only the previous week from Hungary had now settled down.

At least he was no longer fighting for freedom or attempting to kick down his stall as he had done on arrival.

The Prince decided, because his own feelings were somewhat disturbed this morning, that he would ride Aspád, as this horse had been named.

He was just about to open the stable door of his stall when, breathing heavily from the speed with which he had hurried, his Head Groom joined him.

"Good marnin', Your 'Ighness," he said respectfully. "Oi wasn't expectin' ye so early!"

"I know, Barton," the Prince replied, "but it is a lovely morning, and I need some exercise."

He knew as he spoke that all his servants thought it extraordinary that however late he went to bed he was always up early and as active and energetic as if he had had eight hours sleep.

The Prince had trained himself to keep his body as strictly under control as his emotions.

He found that when it suited him he could do quite well with three hours' sleep when other men needed double that amount.

"I was thinking, Barton," he said, "that I might ride Aspád this morning. I can see he is far quieter than he was when he arrived."

"That 'e be, Your 'Ighness," his Head Groom replied, "an' a finer 'orse Oi've never seen. Once Your 'Ighness has trained him, he'll be superb!"

"That is what I thought myself," the Prince replied.

He stepped back for Barton to open the door of the stall, but to his surprise the groom paused.

The Prince saw there was a frown between his eyes.

"What is it?" he asked.

"Oi've only just bin told, Your 'Ighness," Barton answered, "that one o' the guests was 'ere this marnin', and as only Job was on duty, an' he's a rather stupid boy, she insisted on riding off on Györgÿ."

The Prince stared at him in astonishment.

"Gyōrgy!" he exclaimed.

"Yes, Your 'Ighness. O'course, if Oi'd'a knowd Oi wouldn't have allowed it. Gyōrgy's a good 'orse, as Your 'Ighness knows, but he ain't the right mount for a lady!"

The Prince knew this was true.

Gyōrgy was the last horse he had broken in himself, but was still very wild and at times almost uncontrollable, and he knew Barton was right when he said he was certainly not a mount for any woman, however experienced.

"I think there must be some mistake, Barton," he said. "Did Jeb say who it was who had asked for Gyōrgy?"

"He didn't know 'er name, Your 'Ighness," Barton replied, "but he said she were very pretty an' much younger than Your 'Ighness's guests usually are."

"Saddle Jóska quickly while I find out from Jeb in which direction the lady has gone."

The Prince strode off, and Barton hurried to Jóska's stall, realising that the Prince knew he had no time to struggle with Aspád.

Jóska, who was one of the fastest and largest horses in the stable, would carry him wherever he wanted to go quicker than any of the others.

The Prince found Jeb carrying a pail of water from the yard.

Jed looked at his master apprehensively, having guessed from what Barton had said to him that he had done something wrong.

"Have you any idea, Jeb," the Prince asked calmly, "in which direction Miss Claye, who is riding Gyōrgy, has gone?"

"Aye, Your 'Ighness."

Jeb put down the pail and pointed towards the far end of the park.

"Oi watched 'er go, Your 'Ighness," he explained, "an' as Gyōrgy were playing up, Oi were afraid 'e moight throw her, but her rode 'im as if she knew what she were a-doin'."

"I hope she does!" the Prince said beneath his breath.

He turned to where Barton was bringing Jóska out from his stable and into the yard.

He mounted quickly and as the huge black stallion started pulling at the reins eager to be off he rode him swiftly across the park in the direction in which Jeb had pointed.

As he went he thought it inconceivable that any young girl should have chosen Gyōrgy to ride, thinking herself capable of handling a horse which had given him a great deal of trouble.

Gyōrgy was not only hard to control but was also inclined to shy at anything which he considered unusual.

The Prince imagined he would find Miss Claye, he could not remember her first name, lying unconscious somewhere on the ground, and that when he had carried her home, he would have to send the grooms in search of Gyōrgy.

He had never thought, never guessed, that anybody wanting to ride his horses would be up so early that Barton would not be there to advise them and prevent any horse that was not safe from being taken from the stables.

He realised it was because Jeb was so stupid that he had not woken Barton to ask his advice, and that the Claye girl, obviously pleased with the horse's looks, had asked to ride him.

When he thought about her he tried to remember what she was like. At least he was quite certain she did not in any way appear to be a 'horsey' type.

He could only hope that when György threw her, which would undoubtedly be as quickly as possible, she would fall on soft ground, preferably in the meadowland where it was unlikely she would break any bones.

It would, however, cause a commotion and upset his house-party. He would have to apologise to the Marquess that through no fault of his own one of his horses had injured his niece.

The Prince reached the end of the park, then giving Jóska his head galloped across a flat piece of land which the stallion took at a speed that would not have been rivalled on any race-course.

The Prince was making for a high piece of ground from the far end of which he could look for several miles over the valley through which ran a small stream.

Reining in Jóska he made him take the sharp incline upwards more slowly, and when they reached the top came to a stand-still.

He looked first near at hand expecting to see a still body lying on the ground and doubtless György careering wildly some distance away.

But there was no sign of either of them, and when he looked further ahead through the trees towards the stream, then a good two miles away, he saw them.

To his surprise, the girl was still in the saddle and she was riding György along the side of the stream.

It looked as if she was trying to find a place to cross it, although why she should wish to do so he had no idea.

There had, however, been a considerably amount of rain during the last month and the stream, usually quite shallow, was swollen to double its size.

Now that he had seen her, the Prince did not waste time speculating what she was about to do, but knew the sooner he reached her the better.

He moved down the incline and having once again given Jóska his head set off at a pace that brought him down into the valley, and only a short distance from Forella in a little over fifteen minutes.

She was still moving along the bank of the stream trying to find a suitable place to cross it. She had reasoned out that because London was north of them it would be best for her to go south.

Although she was completely ignorant of the English countryside and of the extent of the Prince's estate, she thought that the land on the other side of the water looked wilder and less cultivated.

She was obsessed with only one idea, and that was to get away, and she knew she had been extremely lucky in being able to ride a horse that had, she was sure, both the strength and endurance to carry her all day.

She had to draw Györgÿ to a standstill where for the first time she could see to the bottom of the stream and knew that at this point it was not so deep and a horse could wade across it easily.

She turned him towards the water and, as she did so, looked back.

It was then she saw that still some distance away a man was approaching her on horseback.

Instantly she was aware that she was in danger, and without riding any further into the stream she turned Györÿ back in the direction they had been riding before and spurred him.

Györgÿ was only too willing to show off his paces.

But to demonstrate his independence he at first reared up, hoping his rider would fall off his back, and when she did not do so he bucked two or three times before obedient to the spur in his side he set off at a wild gallop.

Watching, the Prince held his breath as the horse bucked, expecting to see Forella crash to the ground.

He also knew how easy it was for an inexperienced rider to be unseated by a horse that was bucking.

When he saw Forella still in the saddle set off in what he knew was a deliberate effort to avoid him, he thought it was a miracle.

This, however, was a challenge to Jóska which he could not ignore.

There was no need for the Prince even to touch him lightly with his whip or use his spurs.

Instead the stallion leapt forward and there was the thunder of his hoofs as he strained every nerve to show his supremacy by overtaking the horse in front of him.

As she heard the Prince approaching, Forella could hardly believe that any animal could outpace the one she was riding.

But however much she urged György on she could hear the man behind her coming nearer and nearer, until at last she knew despairingly that she could not escape.

She went on trying however until at last the Prince on Jóska drew alongside and she realised who had been following her.

It was a relief to see it was only the Prince and not, as she had expected, the Marquess, who would have been sent by her aunt to bring her back.

Because there was no point in going on racing she gradually and, as the Prince noticed, without much difficulty drew György to a trot, then to a walk and the Prince did the same with Jóska.

After the speed at which they had been riding even he was a little breathless as he asked a very different question from what he had intended.

"Where in God's name did you learn to ride like

that?"

Because it was so unexpected Forella gave a little laugh.

"György is magnificent! I saw his name over his stall, so I know he comes from Hungary."

"Of course," the Prince replied. "But I would be interested to know, Miss Claye, where you are going with him."

Forella was just about to say she was going nowhere in particular when she was aware that the Prince had seen the rolled up bundle at the back of her saddle.

There was not much in it, but she had thought she could not leave with absolutely nothing of her own.

Because Jeb had not understood what she wanted, she had herself with some difficulty, because György had been restless, attached it to the saddle.

It was something she was very expert at doing, having so often had to pack almost everything she possessed on a horse, a mule, or a camel when she was travelling with her father.

There was a brush and comb in one saddle pocket, a toothbrush and a sponge and a piece of soap in the other.

Because she was used to travelling light she knew that for a short while at any rate she would not have to buy such necessities out of the very small amount of money she had with her.

Then as she was wondering desperately what she could reply to the Prince he said, and she thought it was extraordinarily perceptive of him:

"If you are running away, as I suspect you are, I think I am entitled to ask you, if nothing else, where you are taking my horse!"

He saw the colour flooding into her face before she replied in a low voice:

"I apologise for . . . stealing him . . . but I . . . swear to you I would have . . . returned him as soon as it was . . . possible for me to . . . do so."

The Prince was silent for a moment. Then he said:

"I wonder if we could talk about this. Although I cannot force you to confide in me, it is something I would ask you to do, if only for György's sake."

Because the way he spoke was neither condemning nor disagreeable but seemed kind and, although she could not explain it, sympathetic, Forella said quickly:

"It would be much easier, Your Highness, if you would . . . pretend not to have seen me, and let me . . . get away."

"Can you imagine how frustrating that would be for me," the Prince asked, "wondering what had happened to you and György and not being able to help you if you were in any trouble?"

There was a sudden light in Forella's eyes as she asked:

"Would you . . . help me if I told you what was . . . wrong?"

"Shall I say," the Prince replied, "that I would try in every way in my power to do what is best for you?"

He felt Forella give a little sigh of relief before she said:

"I was afraid you would be very . . . angry with me for taking György, but I could not believe any horse could go . . . faster than he can."

"Is that why you chose him?"

"How could I resist anything so beautiful? And I was sure he could outdistance any other horse."

"How did you know that . . . ?" the Prince began. Then he stopped.

"Listen, Miss Claye, we have to talk to each other. Will you have breakfast with me at one of my farms which is not far from here?"

Forella hesitated.

He knew she was thinking that perhaps he was seeking an opportunity either to take the horse away from her so that she could not go any further, or by some method force her to return to the Castle with him.

"I am speaking without prejudice," he said, "and as I have already promised that I will help you if I can, I hope you will trust me."

She looked at him and he thought she had very strange eyes.

There was a touch of green in them, although it might have been the reflection of the grass over which they were moving.

"I . . . trust you," she said in a low voice after an obvious pause.

"Thank you," the Prince answered. "The farm is over there."

He pointed to where just in the distance there were some haystacks, and beyond them smoke rising from a chimney.

As he spoke he touched Jóska with his whip and as the stallion swept forward György followed.

As they rode at a fast pace towards the farm, the Prince thought he had never known a woman who could ride so well and who, in some magical way to which he could not put a name, could control a horse as wild as György without appearing to make any effort about it.

Only when they reached the farm and the Prince led the way towards the stables where he had been before did György protest.

He therefore went through his usual routine of shying, rearing and bucking, but the Prince who had already dismounted watched Forella without interfering.

She not only kept in the saddle, but controlled the horse in a manner he could not have bettered himself, at the same time talking to him.

"Come on, boy, you are going to have a nice rest," she said. "I do not want you to be so tired by these gymnastics that you are too exhausted to take me where I want to go."

There was something quiet and almost mesmeric about her voice, the Prince thought, for Györgmy, finding he could not unseat her, suddenly became docile.

He even allowed himself without any further objections to be taken into the stable, and the stable door was shut behind him.

The Prince made no comment, but walked to the farmhouse where already waiting at the door was an apple-cheeked, middle-aged woman who bobbed a curtsy as he reached her.

"Mornin', Your Highness. It's nice to see ye again! Oi were a-hoping it wouldn't be long before ye came to see us."

"And now I am here, Mrs Hickson," the Prince replied, "and I have brought a young lady for breakfast who is as hungry as I am myself."

Mrs Hickson curtsied to Forella and led the way, talking nineteen to the dozen, into a comfortable Parlour with a table in the window which she quickly covered with a clean white cloth.

"Ye've come just at the right time, Your Highness," she was saying. "Me husband killed pig and Oi cured a ham only last week, and Oi knows it'll be to yer liking."

"I am sure it will," the Prince answered, "and I have always said, Mrs Hickson, that nobody on the whole estate can cure a ham better than you can."

With a smile of delight Mrs Hickson hurried from the Parlour and the Prince saw that Forella was standing on tip-toe looking in the mirror over the mantelpiece as she removed her riding-hat from her head.

When she turned round he realised he was looking at her properly for the first time, and he could see how attractive she was. Yet her looks were unusual and different from those of anybody he had ever seen.

It was not only her hair, with touches of gold in it, and the little curls that had strayed from the chignon in which she had tried to keep them in place and seemed to have a life of their own.

It was also that her eyes, which were very large, on each side of her small straight nose, had, as he had noticed in the field, a touch of green in them.

Her eyelashes were very long and while dark at the roots curled upwards and the points were gold.

There was also something else strange about her, which for the moment he could not put a name to.

She gave him a little smile that was one of shyness, then sat down at the table saying as she did so:

"I admit, now that I think about it, to feeling hungry."

The Prince sat down opposite her and said:

"We have a lot to talk about, but first it will make things easier if you will tell me your Christian name."

"Forella."

"And secondly," he went on, "how you can ride better than any woman I have ever seen?"

He paused before he added:

"I came looking for you, expecting to find an unconscious body with Györy careering away so that it would have taken hours if not days to catch him again."

"I have ridden since I was very young," Forella

64

answered after a moment, "but of all the many horses I have ridden, I have never been on one quite as fine as György!"

There was silence. Then she said impulsively:

"I . . . I would have sent him . . . back to you."

"I do not understand why you had to go away in the first place."

Then as if the Prince was feeling for words he added:

"Am I really such a bad host that you had to escape from the Castle so soon after your arrival?"

He spoke lightly, but to his surprise Forella looked out of the window and there was a note of desperation in her voice as she said:

"I . . . I have to . . . go!"

"Why?"

"I would . . . rather not tell you."

"I would prefer to hear from you what has gone wrong rather than to hear it as I undoubtedly shall from your uncle and aunt on my return."

"I do not think they will . . . tell you the . . . truth."

"Then will you not tell me what I should know?"

He was aware that something was very wrong, and he leaned across the table saying in a voice that every woman he had ever met found irresistibly beguiling:

"Please trust me, Forella. I swear that anything you tell me will be in confidence, and I will do nothing to hurt you or make things more difficult than they apparently are already."

Slowly, it seemed to him, she turned her head and raised her long eyelashes.

He was aware that she was looking deep beneath the surface, as if she searched from some reassurance that she could trust him.

It was, the Prince thought, the first time in his life

that any woman had looked at him in such a manner or was obviously debating within herself whether he was as trustworthy as he professed to be.

Then as her strange eyes met his grey ones and they looked at each other for a long moment, it seemed as if Forella was satisfied because she said:

"There is nothing I can do . . . but run away and . . . hide."

"From what?"

"From what happened . . . last night."

"Will you tell me what happened?"

Forella drew in her breath, then after a moment she said in a voice he could hardly hear:

"The . . . Earl of . . . Sherburn came to my . . . bedroom by mistake . . . he thought it was . . . Lady Esme's room."

The Prince stiffened.

It was hard to believe what he was hearing was the truth.

Then as Forella went on he understood.

"I . . . I was asleep," she said, "and when I woke up I was . . . frightened because there was a . . . man in my room. Then before I could . . . say anything . . . Aunt Kathie came in."

The Prince did not need to hear any more.

He knew exactly what had happened and that this was the revenge Kathie Claydon had been planning when he saw the hatred in her eyes as she looked at Esme Meldrum across the Drawing-Room.

It was a revenge which instinctively he had tried to prevent by flattering her and taking her to another room to see the picture he had bought.

But as Forella, a little incoherently, told him what had occurred, he could guess how it was that the Earl had mistaken, as Kathie intended him to do, Forella's room for the one occupied by Esme.

66

And Kathie had been waiting like a cat at a mousehole for him to do so.

"H – how can I m – marry a man I have . . . never even spoken to?" Forella was asking. "That is . . . why I had to . . . run away."

"I can understand your feelings," the Prince said very quietly.

"You . . . understand . . . you really do?"

"Of course I do," he replied, "but where were you going?"

She made a helpless little gesture which was somehow very pathetic.

"I have . . . only been in England for two . . . weeks, but . . . I thought I could find somewhere where I could . . . hide from Aunt Kathie until it was . . . all forgotten."

"And you have some money with you?"

"I . . . have a little."

He knew she was reluctant to tell him, but almost as if he compelled her to do so, she said:

"Nearly five pounds."

"And you really think that would be enough to keep you from starvation?"

"I could . . . find . . . something to do," Forella replied defensively.

"What can you do?"

"I have been thinking about that," she answered. "I can cook, although perhaps no one would employ me without a reference, and I can also speak quite a number of languages, including Arabic."

The Prince was astonished.

"How can you do that?"

"I have travelled in a great many strange lands with my father."

"I am afraid I know nothing about you," the Prince said. "Please tell me, because I am curious about your father and mother who I gather are now dead."

"My father died of typhoid in Naples at the end of February."

She thought there was an expression of surprise on the Prince's face as if he was thinking it extraordinary that she was not in mourning, and she explained quickly:

"Papa asked that no one should mourn for him because he did not . . . believe in death."

She paused before she added:

"In the East where we spent so much time everybody believes in reincarnation. Papa believed that because he and Mama loved each other so much they would meet again in another life . . . . He said love is indestructible and cannot . . . die."

She spoke, the Prince thought, without being in the least self-conscious about saying things which would make most women simper or feel embarrassed.

"So when your father died, you came back to England."

"I would not have written to Uncle George," Forella said, "but our servant did. He had been with us ever since I was a child, and he thought it was the . . . right thing to do."

"Which, of course, it was!" the Prince approved.

"But I have no wish to live the sort of life that Papa always laughed at. He said Society was a lot of nonsense, and consisted of foolish people who competed with each other for bigger and better titles, and wasted their time and energy in gambling, grumbling and gossip."

The way Forella spoke sounded so funny that the Prince could not help laughing.

"I think your father was right. At the same time, there is not much alternative for young ladies like yourself."

"I have no wish to be a 'Young Lady'," Forella said almost crossly. "I want to go on doing the things I did with Papa, only I am not quite certain how I can do them . . . alone."

"What sort of things did you do with your father?"

She gave him a mischievous little smile which told him he would be surprised at what she had to tell him.

"I was born in a Bedouin tent," she answered. "I have tried to find the source of the Ganges and have climbed the lower slopes of the Himalayas. I have encountered the Head Hunters in Sarawak and have dined with a tribe in Africa whose favourite dish was 'roast Christian'!"

The Prince stared at her incredulously and she laughed at the expression on his face.

It was a very natural sound, he thought, the spontaneous joyous laughter of a child.

"You did ask me," she said before he could speak, "but you do not have to believe me!"

"I think I would know if you were lying," the Prince answered.

"Why should you say that?"

"I have an instinct for such things and, although it seems incredible, I know that you are telling me the truth."

"Then if you believe me, you will know that I have no wish to spend my life with people who are concerned mainly with how unkindly they can speak about one of their friends who is not present."

The Prince's lips twitched, but he said:

"I think that is a rather cruel condemnation."

"Besides which," Forella went on in a different tone, "I hate doing nothing but sitting about all day in overheated, overscented rooms, trying on clothes, and eating at regular intervals."

She paused before she asked:

"Have you any idea how much people like Uncle George and Aunt Kathie eat every day? If you put it all in a bucket it would feed hundreds of starving children in India."

She spoke almost passionately and the Prince said:

"I can understand that you are finding it all somewhat of a shock. At the same time, not everybody in the *Beau Monde* is quite as bad as you are making them out to be."

Forella gave a little shrug of her shoulders before she said:

"I have wanted to get away ever since I came to live in England, and now I *have* to go! You must understand that."

"You do not think that marrying the Earl of Sherburn would give you a position in Society which most young women would think a very enviable one?" the Prince asked.

"That is what Uncle George said to me, and the answer is 'no!' How could I possibly marry a man if I did not love him? Anyway the Earl is in love with somebody else!"

The Prince did not attempt to argue the point.

"The whole idea of being married because Aunt Kathie wishes to be rid of me is degrading and disgusting," Forella went on. "In any case, I do not want a position in Society . . . or to be a puppet pulled by strings to say the right thing, do the right thing, and think what I am told to think! I want to be free . . . I want to be myself!"

"And you are sure that is quite impossible in the environment in which your uncle and aunt live?"

The Prince asked the question seriously, and to his surprise, instead of glaring aggressively at him, Forella thought before she replied:

"That is the sort of question Papa and I used to discuss. I think that one can be oneself anywhere in the world as long as one is not constrained into doing things which one knows to be wrong."

There was silence for a moment before she went on:

"Papa said all living is a search for the development of oneself, and because he and Mama were so blissfully happy together, it did not matter what discomforts they suffered, because they could laugh at them, and every day was one of discovery."

"What did they expect to find eventually?" the Prince asked.

"I suppose the real answer to that is their Souls," Forella replied.

She spoke quite simply, and again the Prince thought it strange that anyone could say such things without seeming to be embarrassed about it.

Then before he could reply the door opened and Mrs Hickson came into the room carrying a tray loaded with food.

A little later Forella said:

"Papa used to tell me how delicious English eggs and bacon were for breakfast. This is the first time I have tasted them really fresh, and I now know what he meant."

As she spoke she helped herself to another piece of new bread warm from the oven and spread it with the golden butter which the Prince knew came from the herd of Jersey cattle that the Hicksons kept.

He poured himself out another cup of tea before he said:

"I think, Forella, we should now get back to the all-important question of what you are about to do."

"You have already agreed that I should go away," she said quickly.

"I said that I understand why you wish to do so."

71

"But you will not stop me?"

"I suppose that is what I really should do," he replied.

She put down what she was eating and said in a very different tone:

"After bringing me here, you could not be so treacherous when I trusted you!"

"Which I hope you will continue to do," the Prince said. "At the same time you must see that what you are contemplating is quite impossible."

"I will make it possible, and you have no right to interfere with me."

"I do not wish to do so, but I can appreciate better than you can the difficulties that lie ahead."

"I have overcome difficulties before."

"Not alone!"

This was irrefutably true and she was silent as he went on:

"For a woman alone in the countryside there are dangers too many for me to enumerate, and undoubtedly somebody would steal György from you, and you would find it hard without money and on your own to get any sort of accommodation."

"Why should I believe that?" Forella asked in a hostile voice.

"Because it is true in England," the Prince replied.

"Then the sooner I get out of this country, the better!" Forella said. "Perhaps the best thing I could do would be to live abroad."

"What I am going to suggest is easier than that," the Prince said. "I realise that you cannot turn to your father's relatives for assistance, but surely there must be some relatives of your mother's somewhere in the country?"

There was silence for a moment before Forella said abruptly:

"My mother was not English!"

To her surprise the Prince exclaimed:

"I was right! I felt there is something about you which is different. Now I know what it is, and unless I am very much mistaken, your mother was Hungarian!"

"Why should you say that?"

"Because no one could ride as well as you do if they did not have Hungarian blood in their veins, and there is something about your face which has puzzled me, and now I know what it is."

"Yes, Mama was Hungarian," Forella admitted, "but Aunt Kathie said I was to tell no one she was a foreigner because it was a disadvantage which might make men unwilling to marry me!"

The Prince put back his head and laughed.

"I have never heard anything so ridiculous! And I suppose you know that I am Hungarian?"

"Yes, of course."

"Then why did you not tell me about your mother?"

"I did not think you would be interested."

"But of course I am! What was her name before she married your father?"

"Rákózi, but I do not suppose you have heard of them. Her family came from East Hungary."

"Of course I have heard of them," the Prince said. "They are a very famous Hungarian family and, as it happens, their lands march with mine."

"Mama ran away with Papa, so if you are thinking of that, the Rákózis will certainly not welcome me!"

"I doubt if that is a fact," the Prince said. "At the same time, it would take us such a long time to find out their feelings in the matter that I have a very different suggestion to make."

"What is it?" Forella asked.

She spoke slowly and with a suspicious look in her

eyes which told him she was afraid he was going to be difficult and somehow prevent her from escaping, as she intended to do.

He seemed to himself to be able in some strange way to read her thoughts, and knew she was thinking that if she could slip away when he was off his guard, she might take Györy from the stables and get away without his being aware of it.

He could almost see in the clearness of her eyes the thoughts going through her mind. Then he said very quietly:

"We both have Hungarian blood in us, Forella, and even though I was prepared to help you before, I now consider I am honour bound to do so, as a fellow countryman."

"You . . . you will help me?"

She was still not sure of him, but he thought there was a little flicker of light and hope in her eyes that had not been there before.

"I realise," the Prince said slowly, "that it would be impossible for you, feeling as you do, to marry the Earl of Sherburn, even though from a social point of view it would be a very brilliant, if unexpected, marriage."

"But . . . he is in love with Lady Esme," Forella said.

The Prince secretly thought there was a more appropriate word for the feeling between the Earl and Esme Meldrum, but Forella, despite her wanderings over the world, was too innocent to understand it.

"It would certainly be a very unhappy way for you to be married," he said, "and it is your feelings that matter to me. I am therefore going to suggest to you, Forella, an alternative to going off on your own in an unknown country, and having to face many dangers and privation even the possibility of starvation with

74

only five pounds in your pocket!"

"If you are thinking of speaking to Aunt Kathie, I can tell you now she will not listen!" Forella said quickly. "She wants to get me married so as to be rid of me, and I think, although I may be mistaken, that she also wants to punish the Earl in some way by making him take a wife."

"Did you think that out for yourself?" the Prince enquired. "Or did somebody tell you that is what your aunt wanted to do?"

"I have been thinking it out since the way she looked at me last night and the note in her voice," Forella replied. "I do not know why, but I am sure she was angry with him not only because he was in my bedroom, but for some other reason."

Now that the Prince had learned that she was Hungarian, he knew that her instinct was as strong as his.

But there was no point in saying so, and he merely said:

"What I am going to suggest to you, and I know you will find it much safer and more comfortable than what you were contemplating, is that you should hide in a house I own which is about five miles across country from here."

"A house?" Forella asked.

"I have a relative of mine living in it," the Prince replied, "who because she is partially crippled lives very quietly and alone in a house I bought her five years ago, when she first came to England from Hungary."

"She is Hungarian?"

"As I said, she is one of my relatives."

"And . . . I could stay with her?"

"I think she would be delighted to have you. She does not speak English very well, and in fact knows nothing of the social life in this country which you find so irksome. She is, however, a well-read, extremely intelligent person, and I think you two would get on very well together."

Forella stared at him. Then she asked:

"Are you really offering me sanctuary in your house, and you will not tell Uncle George or Aunt Kathie where I am hiding?"

"I will give you my word that I will not tell anybody where you are or that we have even met each other this morning, and when it is learned at the Castle that you have disappeared I shall pretend to be extremely surprised!"

"What about the groom? He will tell them that I have taken György."

"Leave him to me," the Prince said. "I will think of some explanation – perhaps that György has been found wandering in the fields, and I have left him in the care of one of my friends."

He smiled before he added:

"I expect you would like to be able to ride him while you are at Ledbury Manor."

"Is that the name of the house to which I am going?"

The Prince nodded.

Forella clasped her hands together.

"Can you really be so . . . kind . . . so . . . understanding," she asked. "I do not know how to begin to thank you."

"As I have already said," the Prince replied, "a Hungarian calling to another Hungarian for help is something which is never ignored."

"Thank you . . . thank you!"

The Prince took his watch from his waistcoat pocket.

"As it will take us a little time to reach Ledbury

Manor," he said, "I think we should start immediately. I must be back at the Castle for breakfast and to face the music when your disappearance is reported."

There was a hint of mischief in Forella's eyes as she said:

"There will certainly be one person who will be delighted at my disappearance and will hope I am conveniently dead, and that is the Earl of Sherburn!"

The Prince laughed before he said:

"I am not going to deny that. Osmond Sherburn has said for years that he has no intention of getting married."

"He will be glad and Aunt Kathie will be very angry!"

"My cousin will look after you," the Prince promised, "and incidentally her name is Princess Maria Dábas."

Forella gave him an enchanting smile as she said:

"It seems almost fate, does it not, that Mama left home and everything that was Hungarian to be with Papa, and now I am going back again, to be saved from what would undoubtedly be hell for me by an Hungarian."

"As you say," the Prince replied, "I think, Forella, fate is playing a very decisive part in your life."

"But of course," Forella said quietly, "and I shall believe in my Karma instead of being so frightened. I am now feeling rather ashamed of myself."

"I can only say it was understandable," the Prince replied. "And now, come and show me once again how well you can handle György."

Without meaning to, as he rose from the table he held out his hand to her as if she was a child.

As she slipped hers into it he thought that from a social point of view he was behaving very reprehensibly.

But his instinct and his Hungarian perceptiveness told him not only was it right, but there was actually no alternative.

4

They had ridden for some way before the Prince said:

"I have been thinking about a new identity for you."

"Of course, that is important," Forella agreed.

"I think the best thing, and certainly the most plausible," he said, "is to say that you are the daughter of a Hungarian friend who is coming to stay with me."

"Hungarian?" Forella interrupted.

"I am going to suggest that you take your mother's name," the Prince said, "and unless I am mistaken, she had a title."

"She was a Countess," Forella confirmed, "but of course she never used it."

"Now it will come in useful," the Prince said. "You will be the Countess Forella Rákózi."

Forella laughed.

"But I am trying to escape from Society and all its glittering baubles!"

The Prince smiled.

"On this occasion you must accept such frivolities! I suppose you can speak Hungarian well enough for people not to question your nationality?"

"You insult me!" Forella replied. "My mother usually spoke Hungarian when we were alone because she said she wished to keep in practice, and Papa spoke it so well, as he did many other languages, that Mama said no one would believe he was not a true Magyar!"

She spoke with a defiant little note in her voice which the Prince had heard before and which he knew meant she expected him to argue with her.

Instead he said almost humbly:

"I apologise."

"I think you are laughing at me," Forella said, "but I have so few possessions of my own that my intelligence is very precious to me."

It was such an original remark that the Prince laughed again.

He thought that his cousin who, as he had said, was a very intelligent woman, would find Forella a relief in what was for the present a somewhat monotonous existence.

"Now we must straighten all this out in our minds," he said, "so that we both tell the same story."

He knew Forella was listening intently as he went on:

"You set out a month or so ago from Hungary to come to England to stay with me, but when you reached Trieste your father died there."

Forella realised he was keeping as near as possible to the truth of what had happened.

"So you came to England alone," the Prince continued, "and since you are in mourning, you have no wish to be in London but would rather stay quietly in the country, which is where I am taking you."

"It is a very good and very convincing story," Forella cried, "and I will be careful to remember my new name."

"I am sure that will be no difficulty," the Prince replied, "and when we arrive I want you to write a note to your uncle."

"A note?"

The fear was back in Forella's eyes.

"Only to tell him that you have run away to stay with some friends," the Prince said quickly, "that you are quite safe and he has no need to worry over you."

She did not speak and after a moment he added:

"Otherwise, if you just disappear, there is every likelihood that your uncle will send the police or certainly detectives in search of you."

Forella gave a cry of horror.

"That must not happen."

"No, of course not," the Prince agreed. "Which is why it is important for you to write a note on which, naturally, there will be no address."

"I think you are being very clever," Forella said, having thought it over, "and I am very . . . very grateful."

She thought as she spoke that only an Hungarian could have entered into a plot so competently, and at the same time understood that she could not go back and marry the Earl of Sherburn.

Then since the Prince had little time to spare if he was to get back to the Castle at a reasonable hour, he rode quickly, and as the horses galloped side by side, it was impossible to talk.

They had crossed the river after leaving the farm, and now Forella was aware that the countryside through which they were riding was, as she had expected, wilder and less inhabited than was the neighbourhood of the Castle.

There was only the occasional farmhouse to be seen in the distance, and they rode for some way on what seemed entirely uninhabited land before the Prince said:

"There is Little Ledbury ahead of us!"

For a moment Forella could see only trees, and then a few thatched roofs amongst them.

As she rode on she discovered a small village in which black and white cottages with their thatched roofs looked like something out of a fairy-tale.

Each cottage had a little garden in front of it brilliant with flowers, and except for a small bow-windowed shop looking onto the village green, there was little else in the village apart from the small grey stone church.

As if she had asked the question the Prince said as they passed it:

"It was built in the 17th century, and is one of the best examples of the period in England."

About fifty yards from the church they turned in through a gate with heraldic lions in stone on either side of it, and when Forella saw Ledbury Manor she realised it had been built at the same time as the church.

Also of grey stone with pointed gables and high chimney-pots, it was very beautiful and over the entrance there was a stone plaque commemorating its first owner with the date '1623' beneath it.

It was not very large, although it was built with three storeys, with diamond-paned windows, and on one side of it was a high wall.

What made it especially dream-like was that perched on the roof and the tables and fluttering round the courtyard was a large number of white doves.

They were so pretty that Forella gave an exclamation of delight and said:

"Doves! The attendants of Aphrodite!"

The Prince, however, did not answer, and there was an expression on his face she did not understand.

But there was no time to ask questions. As they

dismounted from their horses two grooms appeared, who saluted the Prince respectfully and led the horses away to the stables that could just be seen beyond some trees.

Györgÿ attempted to play up, but he was obviously not so fresh after travelling at the fast speed set by Jóska, and the groom soon quietened him.

Forella, however, watched him anxiously and the Prince said:

"He will be all right. Thomas is a very experienced man or I would not have put him in charge of the stable here."

He made it sound as though there were quite a number of horses at the Manor, and as they walked into the house Forella wondered why if his cousin was partly crippled horses were of any great importance.

But she was feeling too apprehensive to ask any questions or to think of anything but her new identity.

The Prince having greeted the Butler said to her:

"I am sure you would like to tidy yourself and it would be best for me to see my cousin alone before I introduce you."

"Yes, of course," Forella agreed.

The Prince turned to the Butler.

"Newman, will you arrange for your wife to look after my guest?" he asked. "Then bring her down to the Drawing-Room where I expect I shall find Her Highness."

"I'll see to it, Your Highness," Newman replied.

He led the way up the stairs and by the time they had reached the top an elderly woman was waiting for them.

She gave Forella a respectful little curtsy, and said:

"Welcome, Ma'am, it's very pleasing for us to see

83

His Highness here again."

She did not wait for Forella to answer, but led the way into a very attractive bedroom with chintz curtains covered in flowers.

The windows looked out over a beautifully kept garden which Forella could see led down to a small stream.

Mrs Newman was talking all the time she was helping Forella to take off her riding hat, then the jacket of her habit.

"It's very hot, Ma'am," she said, "and Her Highness'll understand that you'll feel more comfortable in your blouse."

It was, in fact, a very pretty blouse which the Marchioness had bought and had, Forella thought at the time, been exceedingly expensive.

Of white lawn and inset with real lace, the shop assistant had assured her that it had just come from Paris, as had the habit which was very French, being made of green pique edged with white braid.

"It is something in which you certainly could not follow the hounds," the Marchioness had exclaimed. "At the same time, women who want to ride in the summer are allowed to deck themselves out like peacocks, and you will certainly attract attention, if nothing else!"

Because she had been too busy in simply making her escape to think about clothes, it was only now that Forella remembered she had only one gown in the roll that she had attached to György's saddle.

She thought it best, however, not to mention what she had brought with her until she knew that the Prince's cousin would have her to stay.

She therefore washed her face and hands and Mrs Newman tidied her hair.

Then feeling a little self-conscious she walked to

the top of the stairs, to see Newman waiting for her in the hall.

Only as she went down towards him did she pray that there would be no slip-up in the Prince's plans at the last moment, so that after all she would have to set out on her own.

Now she thought of it she realised how frightening it would be.

When she had run away in sheer panic she had not had time to think out the details or even to decide how she would manage with György and only a very little money between her and starvation.

'The Prince is right, and he is very . . . very . . . kind,' she thought as she reached the Hall.

Then she wondered with a sudden fear if by the time she reached him he might have changed his mind.

But as she was shown into the low-ceilinged, attractive Drawing-Room with the sunshine coming through the casement windows in a golden flood, she knew as he rose to his feet that all was well.

As if he was aware of what she was feeling he crossed to her side and taking her hand, said:

"Cousin Maria, this is Forella Rákózi whom I have been telling you about."

He spoke in Hungarian and the Princess held out her hand saying as she did so in the same language:

"You poor child, I am so sorry for you, and of course you can stay here with me for as long as you wish. It will be delightful for me to have somebody who can speak my own language."

Forella curtsied and said:

"It is very gracious of Your Highness!"

She saw as she looked at the Princess that she had once been very beautiful and still in her old age had a distinction that came from her personality and character.

Instinctively Forella was drawn to her and she was almost sure the Princess felt the same.

Then as she sat down the Princess said:

"You are very lovely, and it is not surprising, for the Rákózis are noted for their beautiful women, are they not, János?"

"So I have always heard," the Prince replied, "and I am certainly ready to agree with what you say."

"You flatter me," Forella said, but her eyes were twinkling in a way which told the Prince that she was amused by his play-acting.

"I am afraid you may find it dull here," the Princess said to her, "but János tells me you are in mourning and that you wish to be very quiet."

"That is what I hope to find," Forella answered, "and I can only thank you for having me as your guest."

"I should be thanking you," the Princess replied "for I cannot pretend that the place is a whirl of gaiety!"

She looked rather reproachfully at the Prince as she spoke, but he laughed.

"You are trying to make me feel sorry for you, Cousin Maria," he protested, "but you know as well as I do that your doctors have told you to rest and, apart from other reasons, for the moment at any rate, this is the right place for you to be."

As if she felt he was reproaching her the Princess put her hand on his arm and said:

"I am not really grumbling, János, and you know I can never thank you sufficiently for all you have done for me."

"Now you are making me embarrassed," the Prince protested, "and I am going to leave Forella with you while I return to look after my house-party."

"Is it the usual collection of pleasure-seeking, beautiful women, and women-seeking handsome men?" the Princess enquired.

The Prince laughed.

"I could not describe it more accurately!"

He kissed her hand. Then he said:

"Forgive me if I take Forella with me for a moment into the Morning-Room. She has some addresses to give me of people I have to contact on her behalf."

"Yes, of course," the Princess replied, "and I am sure you will find everything you want. If not, Newman will be able to provide it."

Forella rose to her feet as the Princess added:

"When shall we see you again?"

"Quite soon," the Prince answered. "Perhaps before I return to London when the party is over."

"I shall be delighted!" the Princess replied.

She sat back in her chair to watch Forella walk with the Prince towards the door.

Then she picked up the newspaper she had been reading before she had been interrupted and carefully studied the Court Circular for her cousin's name.

*   *   *   *   *

The Prince and Forella went into the Morning-Room and when he had shut the door he said:

"Write the letter to your uncle, and I also require you to give me your measurements."

"My measurements?" Forella exclaimed in surprise.

"I cannot believe you expect to wear what you have on day after day without a change," he replied, "and for once I imagine it to be true when a woman says she has 'nothing to wear'!"

"I had really forgotten about clothes," Forella said, "and I suppose the Princess will think it strange if I do not have any."

"Very strange!" the Prince answered, "and I must therefore send for some from London."

There was a pause, and a faint colour came into Forella's cheeks as she said uncomfortably:

"I . . . feel it is an . . . imposition."

"What you are really saying," the Prince said, "is that it is unconventional, but everything you are doing, and have done so far, Forella, has been very unconventional, and it is no use straining at a gnat and swallowing a camel!"

Forella gave a little chuckle and he knew she was thinking of the camels she had ridden and how unpredictable and usually bad-tempered such animals were.

It was strange, he thought once again, how he could read her thoughts and he liked the way she replied:

"You are helping me because you are Hungarian. Perhaps one day, as an Hungarian, I will be able to help you."

"Shall I say that I do not look on it as a debt," the Prince, "but as a responsibility simply because the unfortunate circumstances in which you find yourself happened in my house."

"The person who got me into such a mess is the Earl of Sherburn," Forella flashed, "and it should actually be his responsibility, and not yours."

The Prince smiled:

"I think, however, you are not prepared to point out to him what is his duty."

Forella gave a little cry that was half serious and half joking.

"I will write the note," she said, "and will pray as I do so that Uncle George will believe I am all right, and will not send detectives searching for me."

There was a writing-desk in the window, and she sat down and took a piece of writing-paper from a leather holder which she noticed bore the Prince's insignia.

Then she found lying beside the blotter a pair of jewelled scissors with which she cut off the address from the top of the writing-paper.

Carefully she wrote what the Prince told her to do.

"Dear Uncle George,

I have gone away because it is impossible for me to marry the Earl of Sherburn when he has no wish to marry me.

The only thing I can do is to disappear so that nobody will know what happened, and it will be easy for them to forget I ever existed. I am staying with friends and am quite safe, so please do not worry about me or try to find me.

Thank you for all your kindness for which I am very grateful.

I remain your affectionate niece,

Forella."

Once she had written the note she read it through to see that there were no mistakes, before she held it out to the Prince who was standing with his back to the fireplace.

He took it from her, then handed it back saying:

"Very good! But be careful to put it into an envelope without a crest on the back."

Forella found one in the blotter, put the note inside it, and sealed it down.

Then she wrote on another piece of paper her measurements, which after so many fittings in London she knew exactly.

She rose from the writing-desk and handed both the note and the paper to the Prince as she said:

"I am afraid I have nothing with me except one

dress and a nightgown, but please do not spend too much money or it will take me a long time to pay you back."

"I thought I had already made it clear that what I send you is a gift," the Prince said, "but I am wondering whether you would prefer to be dressed as an English débutante, or as an Hungarian."

"There is no need for me to answer that," Forella smiled. "All the same I was very happy in the clothes I wore with Papa which Aunt Kathie said were fit only for the dustbin, which was where she put them!"

"I understand exactly what you are trying to say to me," the Prince replied, "but I have always believed that a beautiful picture deserves a beautiful frame."

"Now you are talking exactly like an actor in a play," Forella said. "I thought last night when I was at the Castle that the whole thing was not real, but was taking place on a stage!"

She thought he looked surprised and went on:

"It amused the audience but they did not believe for a moment that the actors and actresses were real or projecting anything that actually came from their hearts."

The Prince realised incredulously that she was mocking him and he replied:

"I am just wondering, Forella, why you should set yourself up as critic, judge and jury, and on whose authority you consider yourself justified in putting forward such preposterous suppositions."

For a moment there was silence. Then Forella said humbly:

"You are . . . quite right. I am being . . . impertinent . . . and I am . . . sorry! I forgot for the . . . moment that I was not . . . speaking to Papa. We used to duel with each other in words and . . . always tried to . . . score points off . . . each other."

As she spoke she blushed and the Prince felt he had not only been cruel but unsportsmanlike to one so young and vulnerable and, as he was now aware, very sensitive.

"I like duelling, as you call it, with you," he said quickly, "and it is something I have not done in the same way with anybody else."

He thought she was not appeased and said:

"I want you to go on being frank with me and saying what you think. I do not believe the Social World in which I live is as depraved as you make it out to be, but I have to acknowledge there is a modicum of truth in what you say."

She did not reply, and he realised he had driven the smile from her lips and the mischief from her eyes, and asked himself how he could have been so clumsy.

At the same time he was even more aware than he had been before that she could never cope with the world on her own.

When he said goodbye Forella thanked him once again and her gratitude was very sincere.

As she stood on the steps and watched him mount Jóska who had been brought from the stables, the Prince felt as he took a last look at her that she looked very young and very much alone.

As he rode on he hoped he had done the right thing in helping her as she had asked him to do.

At the same time he was aware that he had taken a heavy responsibility upon himself, and had behaved in a manner which most people would think extremely reprehensible.

After all, in the Social World no young girl could ask more than to be the wife of the Earl of Sherburn, whatever the circumstances that obliged him to make her his bride.

The Prince knew that in England, as in most

countries, the daughters of aristocrats had no choice as to whom they married.

Marriage was in fact exactly the same sort of bargaining contract which had begun in Roman times and which meant a business exchange of money or land.

It was assumed that just as royalty married royalty, so aristocrat should marry aristocrat and blue blood marry blue blood.

Despite the fact that Kathie had tricked Osmond Sherburn into marrying her niece, the Prince knew the Marquess would ultimately think it an excellent match from Forella's point of view and from his own.

"I suppose if I thought like an Englishman and did what an Englishman does," the Prince told himself, "I would either have forced Forella to come back with me to the Castle, or would now behave in what she would consider a treacherous manner and tell Claydon where she is."

But he was not English, he was Hungarian, and having given Forella his word, he would not break it.

"Besides," he tried to appease his conscience, "she is very different from the ordinary English débutante, which of course is because she is half Hungarian."

He arrived back at the Castle before nine o'clock, at which time he knew the gentlemen in the house-party would be gradually staggering downstairs for breakfast.

The ladies would ring much later for their maids, the majority of them not appearing before lunchtime.

It was therefore quite easy for the Prince as he walked towards his bedroom to leave the note Forella had written for her uncle on a table in the corridor outside her room.

It was unlikely, he thought, that it would be found and taken to the Marquess until much later, by which time he would have told Barton that he had seen no sign of György or the horse's rider, and had therefore returned to the Castle, hoping they had come back by another route.

Having seen Barton he wrote to a dressmaker in Bond Street with whom he had spent large sums of money in the past.

He went into the Library where, as he expected, most of his male guests were congregated reading the newspapers.

Among them was the Marquess who bade him good-morning in a quite ordinary tone of voice.

The Prince thought, with satisfaction, that he and his wife must have arranged for 'the fireworks' to be let off later on.

There was no sign of the Earl and it was an hour or so later that the Prince learned that he had gone out riding accompanied by Lady Esme.

One of the reasons why the Prince's parties were always such a success was that he made it clear that his guests could do exactly as they wished, and every facility was provided for their amusement.

There were horses and carriages available for them to ride or drive, there were boats on the lake, two croquet greens, several tennis courts and he had recently installed a covered court, which was a delight when it was raining.

There was also a golf course and inside the Castle the inevitable Billiard Room.

As the Prince thought of the Earl and Lady Esme he found himself anticipating what their conversation would be, and thought that later in the day the Earl was in for a pleasant surprise.

*   *   *   *   *

As they rode slowly through the woods in which the

rides had been cut exactly wide enough for two horses to move side by side, the Earl was saying:

"What am I to do, Esme? What the hell am I to do about it?"

"I think it is so disgraceful of Kathie to behave in such an underhand manner," Lady Esme exclaimed, "that I feel I can never speak to her again."

She was looking exquisitely beautiful, at the same time a little pale due to the fact that she had lain awake half the night wondering why the Earl had not come to her as he had promised he would.

When she had received a note from him soon after she was called she had known even before she read it that something was very wrong.

"I must see you immediately, and I suggest we go riding. I will be waiting in the stables in half-an-hour's time."

It was difficult for Esme to dress so quickly, even with the help of her very experienced lady's-maid but somehow she managed it.

When she joined the Earl and raised her blue eyes reproachfully to his, she was astounded by the expression on his face.

Although it seemed impossible, he appeared to have aged considerably since she last saw him, and there was a grimness about the tightness of his lips and the darkness of his eyes which she did not understand.

Only when he had told her what had occurred did she give a cry of anger and frustration that made him want to hold her in his arms and comfort her.

"It is diabolical! Absolutely diabolical! Kathie is a devil to plan anything so cruel and wicked!"

"It is my fault," the Earl said. "We should not have used the Prince of Wales's signal, which has been laughed about in every Club and, I suspect, in every

Boudoir."

"There were no roses in the vase in my room," Esme explained, "so I put a lily outside the door instead."

It flashed through the Earl's mind that the choice of flower would have made Kathie sneer and perhaps make her feel even more angry than before.

He was aware that while Kathie had taken a number of lovers since she had begun to be unfaithful to her husband, he would have been Esme's first, and therefore the lily was in some ways appropriate.

"If only I could have come to you, darling, last night after it had happened and told you all about it," he said. "It would have been better than having to go to my own room and be alone with all the demons of hell taunting me for being caught in a trap!"

"That is exactly what it was," Esme exclaimed indignantly, "a trap set by Kathie! I hate her, Osmond, do you hear me? I hate her!"

"I feel very much the same way," the Earl admitted. "The question is, how can I prevent myself from being marched up the aisle to marry her niece when all I want is to remain a single man?"

As he finished speaking he thought it sounded rather impolite, and added quickly:

"And be with you, my lovely one!"

"That is what I want," Esme said softly, "but after all, Osmond, darling, if you are married, as I am married, it will not really make very much difference!"

*   *   *   *   *

It was not until nearly lunchtime that the Marchioness, putting the finishing touches to her appearance, said to her maid:

"Jones, go and tell Miss Forella I wish to speak to her, and if she has gone downstairs already tell one of the servants to find her."

"Very good, M'Lady," Jones said, "but as I haven't heard her moving, I expects she's still asleep."

"Then wake her up!" the Marchioness said sharply.

She was, however, smiling as she looked at her reflection in the mirror.

She had certainly made the Earl pay for his treatment of her.

She had also made quite certain this morning before George went down to breakfast that he would not go back on his decision that the Earl must marry Forella.

"It was damned careless, if you ask me, for Sherburn to go bursting into the wrong room," the Marquess had said. "At the same time, this place is like a rabbit warren."

"As you say, George," his wife replied, "it was extremely careless. But whatever the reason, it would be a great mistake for poor little Forella to suffer."

She took a quick glance at her husband to see if he was listening and went on:

"You know as well as I do that if there was the slightest whisper about his going to her bedroom, let alone being seen leaving it, the child would be ostracised by all the important hostesses.

She paused to add impressively:

"We could never, never, by any possible means, find her a husband who would overlook such a thing!"

"All right, Kathie, I know what you are saying," the Marquess answered irritably. "At the same time, I like Osmond, and I feel it is rather caddish to throw him a back-hander!"

"Whatever you may or may not think, George," the Marchioness replied, "it is some satisfaction to know that with Osmond's fortune you will have no need to give Forella a dowry. He can well afford to look after his wife."

"I was not thinking about money," the Marquess retorted. "I am thinking about Sherburn, and of course Forella! She will be no more able to cope with him than a babe in arms!"

He did not wait for his wife's reply but went out of the room shutting the door unnecessarily loudly.

The Marchioness was not perturbed. She merely gave a low laugh and thought that the Earl would be regretting by now that he had ever left her.

Jones, having knocked on the door of Forella's bedroom and receiving no answer, had entered it quietly.

The sunshine was coming through the uncurtained windows, and one glance told her that Forella was not there.

She therefore went to the top of the stairs and, having beckoned one of the footmen on duty in the Hall to come up to her, asked him to go and find Miss Forella.

"I 'ears the maid who looks after 'er say," he answered, "that 'er's gone riding, and hasn't come back."

"Well, she should be back soon," Jones retorted. "Tell her when she does appear that Her Ladyship wants her."

The footman grinned and scuttled back to the Hall again while Jones returned to the Marchioness.

"I've made enquiries, M'Lady," she said, "and it appears Miss Forella's out riding."

The Marchioness glanced at the clock.

"She will be late for luncheon," she said. "Really, how tiresome girls are! An empty place at the table will certainly annoy the Prince."

"There's time yet, M'Lady, for Miss Forella to come

back and change," Jones said soothingly.

By this time, although the Marchioness was not aware of it, a housemaid dusting the corridor had found the note addressed by Forella to her uncle.

She took it down the back stairs to the pantry where the footman who took it from her waited for the Butler, who had gone down to the cellar, to return before he handed it to him.

The Butler then had to put on his tail-coat and find a silver salver, before without hurrying he carried the note through the house to the Library where he knew the Marquess was most likely to be.

By this time the guests were beginning to assemble for luncheon, and just before the Butler brought in the note, first the Earl, then a little later Esme Meldrum joined the other guests.

"You are very energetic, Sherburn," somebody remarked to the Earl. "I had intended to go riding this morning, but what with the late hour at which we went to bed and, I suspect, our host's excellent wine, the effort proved too much for me!"

The Earl murmured a somewhat incoherent reply, then hid himself behind a copy of *The Times*.

As he appeared to be somewhat out of sorts he was left alone.

When Esme appeared the Marchioness said with a false smile:

"How fresh you look! It must be the effect of riding so energetically and so early!"

"It was actually very enjoyable," Lady Esme managed to say in a somewhat affected voice, hoping that her hatred for the Marchioness did not show in her blue eyes.

Then she crossed the room to talk to two other women who had found it far more agreeable to lie in bed than to face the sunshine.

The Butler stopped beside the Marquess and held out the note on the salver.

The Marquess took it wondering why he should receive a letter when he had given instructions to his servants in Park Lane that as he was to be away only for the weekend he did not wish anything forwarded.

He pulled Forella's note out of the envelope, read it, then ejaculated almost beneath his breath:

"Good God!"

He read it again to be quite certain he had not made a mistake before he walked to where his wife was talking animatedly to the Prince and drew her on one side.

"What is it, George?" she asked, thinking it was extremely inconsiderate of him to interrupt at such a moment.

"I have something to show you," the Marquess said quietly.

He took her arm in a determined manner and drew her to a corner of the room where they could not be overheard.

Because there was nothing she could do about it she went with him with an ill grace.

Only when he had handed her Forella's note and she had read it did she stare at the paper as if she could not believe her eyes.

"I thought she had no friends in England," she said at length.

"If she has, I have no idea who they are."

"Then what are you going to do?"

"What can we do?" the Marquess enquired.

The Marchioness folded the note and put it back into the envelope.

Then she said:

"If this is a plot between her and Osmond Sherburn, I will kill him!"

"You cannot make a scene here!" the Marquess said quickly.

"No, of course not," his wife replied, "but I will speak to Osmond after luncheon."

There was certainly no time now for at that moment Newman went up to Lady Roehampton and announced:

"Luncheon is served, M'Lady!"

Lady Roehampton, who had been talking at the other end of the room to the Prince, began to collect the ladies to move into the Dining-Room.

Only as she reached the Marchioness did she say as she was the most important woman present:

"Go ahead, Kathie dear."

"I am afraid, although you will think it very bad manners," the Marchioness said, "that Forella will not be here for luncheon. I can only say how sorry I am for not letting you know sooner, but I will explain afterwards."

Lady Roehampton without making any comment gave instructions to the Butler to remove one place from the table.

As they walked slowly towards the Dining-Room she was wondering how she could rearrange the table so that two men would not be sitting together.

She soon decided it would be impossible but managed instead very skilfully to seat side by side two sportsmen who had a common interest in racing. This meant they had plenty to discuss and did not mind that there was no female between them.

Watching the Earl the Marchioness thought he looked round the table apprehensively as if he was searching for Forella.

She was quite certain it was just a pretence and he was well aware that she had left.

"He has persuaded her to go away so that he can

somehow get out of the engagement," she calculated, "but that is something I will never let him do! He will marry her, even if George has to challenge him to a duel to make him do so!"

She was quite certain it would not come to that, because both the Earl and the Marquess had a horror of scandal or being written about in a derogatory way in the newspapers.

The Marchioness thought she would enjoy every moment of the marriage in which the Earl was the reluctant bridegroom, humiliated by knowing she had the upper hand!

Whatever happened in the future, he would always know that she was laughing at him.

"I have won! I have won!" she told herself triumphantly. "He will regret that he left me every time he looks at the woman who bears his name!"

As the ladies left the Dining-Room she managed as she passed the Earl to say in a voice that only he could hear:

"I must see you, Osmond, it is important!"

She thought he was about to refuse her, but when the gentlemen came into the Library a little later, she moved to his side and said:

"Let us go into the garden. I have something to show you!"

She knew he was longing to walk away from her, and not to listen to what she had to say.

But feeling presumably that it might make things even worse than they were already, he acquiesced with a bad grace.

Because she knew him so well, she was aware what he was feeling without having to look at the squareness of his chin and the hardness of his eyes.

They walked across the green lawn until they were well out of earshot of any of the others who had come out onto the terrace.

Without saying anything, the Marchioness handed him Forella's note.

She waited until he had read it, then she said:

"As this is your doing, I wish to know where you have sent her."

"It has nothing to do with me, and I have no idea where the girl has gone!" the Earl replied sharply.

"Do you expect me to believe that?"

"You may believe what you like," he retorted. "I can only imagine she had the good taste to be disgusted by your behaviour last night, and too shy to relish either your company or mine."

"You are very eloquent," the Marchioness sneered, "but as you can imagine, George is very perturbed as to what has happened to Forella. She has never been in England before. She has no friends, and from all I can gather from the servants, she went riding before breakfast on one of the Prince's horses and has not returned."

For the first time the Earl seemed interested.

"She went alone?"

"Of course she went alone!" the Marchioness snapped. "She knows nobody in the house except for her uncle and me."

"Well, all I can say is she shows a great deal of good sense!"

"Do not talk like that," the Marchioness said angrily. "Tell me where she has gone!"

"I can only repeat that I have absolutely no idea," the Earl answered. "I know nothing about your niece. Except that, as I have already said, I think she has shown a great deal of common sense."

"Are you telling me that is all you have to say in the matter?" the Marchioness queried.

"What do you expect me to say?" the Earl replied.

"Do you want me to call out the hounds and hunt her down as if she were a fox?"

He paused to say slowly:

"As far as I am concerned, she can stay away as long as she likes because, Kathie, one thing is certain: until you can produce her it would be quite useless and would cause a great deal of comment if you announced our engagement!"

There was an expression of satisfaction on the Earl's face which made the Marchioness long to strike him.

Then because she had no answer to what he had said and knew it was the truth, she walked away from him, her bustle moving as she did so, like a tempestuous sea!

5

As Forella dismounted from Györy at the front door,
she said to Thomas who had escorted her on her ride:

"Thank you very much, that was very enjoyable."

"I enjoyed it too, M'Lady," Thomas replied.

As he rode off to the stables he took off his cap and
Forella, walking into the house, thought what a nice
man he was.

She had been afraid when she wished to go riding
on Györy and was aware she must be accompanied
by a groom, that he would slow the pace and
complain if she rode too far ahead of him.

But to her surprise she found the stables of the
Manor contained a dozen exceptionally fine horses,
and that Thomas, who was in charge of them, was
different from what she expected an ordinary English
groom to be.

A good-looking man of about forty, he was, she
thought, better mannered and certainly far better
educated than seemed appropriate to his position in
life.

Of course she had had no experience of English
stables, but she at least knew when a man was an
expert with horses, and there was no doubt that was
what Thomas was.

If she appreciated him, she realised from the first

moment after they had ridden together that he appreciated her.

It would have been impossible for anybody seeing the way she handled György who was usually extremely obstreperous when she first mounted him, not to be aware that she could ride any animal, however wild.

When György was more or less under control Thomas said:

"I congratulate you, M'Lady."

Forella flashed him a smile.

"It is only György's fun," she said, "and I have never enjoyed riding a horse so much or looked forward to riding as much as I am doing this morning."

"I feel sure you will not be disappointed," Thomas said.

He took her for miles and as it was in the opposite direction from where she knew the Castle was situated, she was not afraid of seeing any members of the house-party.

Actually they saw very few people, only some men working in the fields, and sometimes a farmer's gig or farm cart trundling along the narrow lanes.

It was two days later that Forella plucked up enough courage to ask:

"Why does His Highness want so many horses here? And who is there to ride them?"

There was a little pause before Thomas replied:

"Some of them are carriage horses, M'Lady, and the others His Highness leaves with me so that I can break them in when he has not the time to do so himself."

"You have worked for him for long?" Forella enquired.

Again there was a little pause before Thomas replied:

"I have in fact been with His Highness for nearly three years."

It was obvious that Thomas did not wish to be communicative, and she thought it was an intrusion to ask him too many questions.

At the same time, she was curious about him and increasingly so, as the days passed, about a number of other things.

She could not quite understand the organisation of the Manor itself, which she had thought so beautiful when she had first arrived.

Mrs Newman brought breakfast to her in her bedroom suggesting that as the Princess always had breakfast in bed she would be more comfortable upstairs than sitting alone in the Dining-Room.

"It will be very luxurious," Forella had answered.

She was thinking as she spoke that in the last years since her mother's death she had usually got up early to prepare her father's breakfast. Even when they had servants they did not always give him the food he liked.

At other times when they were travelling breakfast had often been cooked over a camp fire or consisted of a native meal of maize and nuts made more palatable with coconut milk.

But whatever it was, even if it was fresh from a tree, Forella always brought it to her father and waited for him to tell her if it was to his liking.

Sometimes, almost as if he was homesick, he would say:

"I am fed up with this food! I want a good English breakfast of eggs and bacon, and a choice from half a dozen silver dishes laid out on a side table as there used to be at home."

Then he would laugh and add:

"I must be growing senile if that is the sort of life I

want! But it is doubtless what will happen to me in my old age."

Then he would talk excitedly of some new country he wanted to explore or an expedition that required a great deal of planning, and invariably cost more than they could afford.

The second morning after she had finished her breakfast Forella heard a soft cooing note at the open window and saw one of the white doves sitting on the ledge, regarding her with a curious eye.

She got out of bed slowly and carefully, so as not to frighten it away and, taking a piece of toast from the silver rack, walked across the room breaking it into small pieces as she did so.

The dove, however, was not in the least frightened and waited for her first to place a small piece of toast in front of him, which he ate, then took the rest from the palm of her hand.

As he flew away Mrs Newman came into the room.

"You've finished your breakfast, M'Lady?" she enquired.

"Yes, thank you," Forella replied, "and what I could not eat one of those lovely white doves gobbled down as if he was not too fat already."

She laughed, but there was a frown between Mrs Newman's eyes.

"I don't think you should feed them here, M'Lady," she said. "They belong to the Poor Lady."

"The Poor Lady?" Forella questioned.

Mrs Newman turned away and picked up the tray.

"No, I'm sure it's all right," she said quickly. "Please forget what I said just now, M'Lady. I made a mistake."

She went from the room before Forella could say any more. But she stared after her thinking it very strange that she was so abrupt and wondering who the 'Poor Lady' could be.

She supposed she was referring to the Princess, but so far she had not seen her feeding the doves.

In fact, Forella remembered only yesterday she had complained about them, saying they made so much noise that they woke her up in the morning, and there was really getting to be too many of them.

"But they are so pretty," Forella had expostulated.

"They may be, but they make a mess," the Princess replied, then started to talk about something else.

But if it was not the Princess, who was the 'Poor Lady'?

Forella had found there were quite a number of servants in the house, many more than she would have expected.

She was very ignorant of how English houses were run, although her father had told her of the great army of servants that his father and her grandfather had employed in their ancestral home in Huntingdonshire.

She could remember how he used to enumerate them for her starting with the scullery-boy and ending with the Groom-of-the-Chambers, who he said was so important that the staff were as frightened of him as they were of their master.

Because he enjoyed talking about his home and his ancestors Forella would beg him to tell her about it.

He would then describe to her in every detail how he had been brought up when he was a small boy, and the big parties which had been given at Claye Park.

When she was alone with her mother she would also encourage her to talk of her life in Hungary, the Palace in which her family lived and the acres of land they owned in the East of Hungary.

It had been a fascinating contrast which she had stored in her memory.

Ever since coming to England she had wished over and over again that her father was with her to make her laugh at all the rules and regulations which he had dispensed with in his life.

But she knew that was what made a house as big as the Prince's Castle run as smoothly as clockwork.

The Manor was very small in contrast, and yet there were mob-capped maids in gingham dresses who cleaned the house in the morning and young footmen with crested buttons on their livery who helped Newman to wait on the Princess at mealtimes.

Forella often wondered what they did when they had finished in the Dining-Room, but she suspected that Newman, who had plenty of authority about him, kept them busy one way or another.

As far as she was concerned every day was an enchantment which she had not expected to find.

There was always the joy of riding immediately after breakfast when the Princess had no wish for her company.

In the afternoon she found herself enjoying every moment of the Princess's conversation which was clever, informative, and at the same time so human and understanding that Forella felt almost as if she was listening to somebody reading her fairy-stories.

It was on Tuesday, when both she and the Princess were hoping that his house-party would have broken up and the Prince would call and see them, that the Princess said:

"Did János tell you about me?"

"He said you were his cousin and that he had given you this house when you came to England."

"He did not say why I had to come here?"

"No."

"Then you might as well know that if there is an archangel on this earth, then it is János Kovác!"

"I had not thought of him quite like that, although he has been very, very kind to me!" Forella said.

"He is kind to everybody," the Princess smiled. "There is nobody who has ever turned to János for help who has not received it, and I lie awake at night wondering why such a man with so much goodness in his heart should not be happy."

"He is not happy?" Forella asked in surprise.

She thought the Princess was about to say something, but suddenly changed her mind to say instead:

"The rich are not always as happy as people imagine them to be."

"Tell me in what way the Prince has been kind to you," Forella asked.

The Princess paused for a moment. Then she said:

"There is no reason why you should not know. As he told you, I am his cousin but from a different generation. I suppose like all Hungarian families the Kovács stick together through thick and thin, except when one of us, as I did, deliberately severs the ties that bind us to each other."

Forella was interested.

"What do you mean?" she asked.

The Princess smiled as she said:

"I married the man I loved!"

And the Kovács did not approve?"

"They disapproved violently, eloquently and furiously!"

"But, why?"

"That is what I will tell you, my dear," the Princess said. "My husband was not an aristocrat – not quite a 'man of the people', but very nearly and he was also a revolutionary."

"How exciting!"

Forella looked at the Princess with wide eyes and as if she enjoyed having such an attentive audience the

110

old lady went on:

"When they threatened to shoot Imbe Dábas if he came near me, I ran away with him."

"How brave of you!"

As Forella spoke she thought perhaps it was easier to run away with somebody one loved than alone, as she had tried to do.

"I crept out one night, just like a character in a romantic novelette," the Princess went on, "carrying everything valuable I possessed wrapped in a shawl. Imbe was waiting for me and we rode away from my father's Palace, knowing that if we were caught Imbe would undoubtedly die, and I should be more or less imprisoned in the Palace with no chance of ever escaping again."

"But you got away!" Forella exclaimed.

"We rode for two days without sleep," the Princess said, "until we were off my father's land. Then we were married."

"Where was that?"

"In a little church at the foot of the mountains."

"And you never regretted running away?"

"Never, never!" the Princess cried. "I loved Imbe, and he adored me. I suppose you could say we were made for each other, and we were only complete, one person, when we were together."

"It sounds very romantic!" Forella said. "And it is what my father and mother felt about each other."

"That is real love," the Princess said, "and whatever happened in the future I knew from the moment Imbe made me his wife that I was the luckiest woman in the whole world."

Her voice as she spoke was very moving, and Forella asked:

"What happened after that?"

"We went on living in Hungary," the Princess said,

111

"but Imbe became notorious as a man who was always attacking the complacency of the Government, asking for reforms, taking up the causes of those who were downtrodden and unjustly treated."

"Did you help him?" Forella asked.

"I helped him by loving him and by keeping his home life completely separate from his public one."

Forella must have looked a little disappointed for the Princess said:

"It was what he wanted. Because I was so precious to him he would not allow me to expose myself in a world where he was constantly abused and also consistently misunderstood."

"I suppose that happens to all reformers," Forella murmured.

"You are right," the Princess said, "and yet, while a great many people decried Imbe and hated him, he did get a great many abuses reformed which would never have happened if he had not fought for those who were too weak to fight for themselves."

"He sounds magnificent!"

"I thought so," the Princess replied. "So it did not matter to me that none of my family would speak to me, and that my so-called friends cut me if they saw me, because there was really nobody in my life except Imbe."

As if she thought Forella did not understand, she said:

"I soon realised that the people who were working with him and who followed his lead looked at me with suspicion."

"Why should they do that?"

"I was one of the 'upper classes' whom they hated, and with a good deal of justification!" the Princess replied simply.

She made an expressive little gesture with her

hands as she added:

"Their attitude did not matter to me any more than my family's for to me there was only Imbe! Imbe who would come home to me and tell me how much he loved me, and I could, in his arms, forget everything else, however troublesome."

There was a smile on the Princess's lips as she said:

"When you get to my age, child, you will realise that the only things that are worth remembering are the times of happiness, and that means the times one gave and received love."

Forella went on to ask her more about the man she had married, and to learn how he had fought valiantly and at times successfully against those who tried to suppress him.

"But they got him in the end," the Princess said sadly. "Some small mistake made by one of the men he trusted gave them a chance to sentence him to death."

"Oh, no!"

Forella gave a cry of horror.

"Yes, they killed my Imbe," the Princess said, "and they would not even allow me to say goodbye to him before he died!"

"That was cruel and heartless!"

"They were afraid that if they allowed him any concessions he would somehow manage to escape at the last moment. He had always led a charmed life, and they had begun to think he was indestructible!"

"It must have been . . . terrible for . . . you!"

"It was thought that I too should be taken to prison," the Princess went on quietly, "and if that happened, I knew that even if I was not publicly condemned to death I should die."

"And the Prince saved you?" Forella asked, as if she knew the answer.

"Yes, János appeared, just when I was desperate, and took me away from Hungary before anybody could realise what was happening, and brought me to England."

She sighed before she continued:

"There was always a chance that the Hungarian Government would ask for my repatriation, so he brought me here to live very quietly, hoping that as nobody had heard of me, and they could not find me, they would soon forget my very existence, and I think that is what has happened."

"It is the most thrilling, exciting story I have ever heard," Forella exclaimed, "and I admire you for your bravery!"

"I do not want to be admired for anything except giving the most controversial man in my country great happiness through all the years we were together," the Princess said simply.

She was silent for a moment before she added:

"Now I want only to die so that I can be with him again."

"Which you will be!" Forella exclaimed. "Papa was always quite certain that when he died he would be with my mother."

"If one loves somebody enough, there is no possibility that one could ever lose them," the Princess said quietly.

Then as if she felt she had talked enough about herself, she said:

"And that is what I would wish for my dear, wonderful János, that he should find love."

"I thought he was married," Forella said.

"He is," the Princess answered. "It was an arranged marriage when he was very young, and it has not brought him happiness."

She spoke in a suppressed way as if she did not wish

114

to say any more, and because Forella was aware of what she was feeling she said tactfully:

"It seems wrong that anybody so handsome and so kind should not be happy. I am sure somewhere there must be a woman waiting for him, as your husband was waiting for you, who will bring him everything he deserves."

"That is what I pray for every morning and every night," the Princess said. "In fact, every time I think of him."

*　　*　　*　　*　　*

When she went to bed that night, Forella found herself thinking about the Prince, and being surprised at learning he was so different from what she had supposed.

Because he was surrounded by socialites like her uncle and aunt, the Earl and Lady Esme, and all the other guests she had met at the Castle, she had thought that although he had been kind to her he only enjoyed the sort of life at which her father had laughed.

"Who wants to go to Buckingham Palace?" he had said once to her mother.

"I would like to go there just once," her mother replied, "and see if it as grand and as glamorous as I have always understood it to be."

"You will see a lot of dressed-up fools," her father replied, "waiting for a Royal smile or a pat on the hand, like a lot of sea-lions waiting for fish."

Her mother had laughed.

"That is very scathing, darling."

"It is the truth," he said. "Men and women who you would think had some brain in their heads would crawl from here to the North Pole for the chance of receiving a Royal favour or, better still, a bit of metal they call a medal to hang on their chests!"

"You are not to talk like that in front of Forella!" her mother protested.

"Why not?" her father asked. "When the time comes, which you are determined it shall, for her to be presented to Her Majesty the Queen, she can make up her own mind if it is the most exciting thing that ever happened to her, or whether she would rather be racing me on a horse who needs exercise along a beach stretching out in front of us."

Her mother had laughed and jumped up to say:

"'We will both race you!"

After that any more talk about Buckingham Palace had been forgotten.

But her father's mockery of it had remained in Forella's mind, and she had come to England feeling prejudiced against the social life she was to lead with her uncle and aunt.

What happened when the Earl of Sherburn had come to her bedroom by mistake had only confirmed her belief that her father had been right and everything to do with Society was unpleasant and even rather frightening.

Now what she had learnt about the Prince made her revise her opinion about him.

"It is because he is Hungarian," she told herself. "I know when I am talking to him that he is perceptive like Mama. He understands what I am feeling, and what I am thinking, as no ordinary Englishman would be able to do."

*   *   *   *   *

The following day something else happened that made her see once again how different the Prince was.

She had been in the garden and had picked some

116

very lovely and heavily scented yellow roses for the Princess.

Carrying them in her hand she was just about to go into the Drawing-Room when she heard somebody talking inside.

She wondered who it could be, and if it would be a mistake for her to intrude.

Then she heard a man say in French:

"Do not worry, *Princesse*, I am glad you called me, but it is nothing serious."

Forella then knew it was the doctor who was with the Princess, and she thought that if he was prescribing for her she should wait outside until he had left.

At the same time, she was surprised he was speaking in French, but supposed it was easier to make himself understood as the Princess was not entirely proficient in English.

Then as she would have turned away from the door she heard him add:

"Poor lady, there is nothing much I can do for her except keep her quiet. I have given her something to make her sleep, and when she wakes she will have forgotten what has happened."

At his words Forella was still.

'Poor lady' were the words that Mrs Newman had used, and if the doctor was prescribing for one of the servants he would not have used that expression.

Because she was curious she walked into the Drawing-Room, and the Princess looked up to say in rather halting English:

"Oh, here you are, my child, I want you to meet Dr Bouvais, who attends me and is always a welcome visitor, professionally or otherwise."

"Your Highness is very kind," the doctor said.

He held out his hand to Forella saying:

"*Enchanté, Mademoiselle.*"

Not only the way he spoke but the way he looked made Forella realise that he was, in fact, French, and she answered him in his own language saying:

"I am delighted to meet you, *Monsieur*!"

"I was told that you were Hungarian," he said in surprise, "but you speak French like a Parisienne."

"That is a compliment he has never paid me!" the Princess said. "My guest, *Monsieur*, is a very talented young lady!"

"And a very excellent rider!" the doctor said. "The whole village is talking of how they have never seen one of the Prince's horses ridden by a lady before."

Forella, who had no idea that anyone had noticed her outside the Manor, hoped it would not be dangerous.

Then she told herself she was sure that the Prince's idea that she should write to her uncle and say she was safe would prevent him from making any enquiries about her.

"I must now leave you, *Madame*," the doctor said.

He kissed the Princess's hand in French fashion, paid Forella a compliment with an unmistakable look of admiration in his eyes, and left.

Forella gave the Princess the roses saying as she did so:

"Surely it is very unusual to have a French doctor in the village?"

The Princess laughed.

"Surely you realise that he is another of dear János's lame ducks?"

"There is some reason for his being in Little Ledbury?"

"Of course," the Princess said. "Practically everybody around here has a reason for burying themselves in this dead-and-alive hole. As you can guess, I am extremely curious as to why you are here."

Forella looked away from her and said quickly:

"Please tell me about the doctor."

"Why not?" the Princess asked. "He makes no secret, to me at any rate, that if it were not for János he would have stood trial in France and doubtless have received a sentence of several years' imprisonment."

"What did he do?" Forella asked.

The Princess shrugged her shoulders.

"He did not tell me the exact details, but my guess is that he performed an illegal operation and it was discovered, or else the patient died."

Forella did not speak and the Princess went on:

"But whatever happened, I am sure he was not really to blame, for a kinder, more considerate man I have never met. He is also very intelligent, and while it is very pleasant for me to have him here, I cannot help feeling he is wasted."

Forella had a great deal to think about when she was alone, and she thought once again that it was rather like a play taking place in front of her eyes, but very different from the one she had watched at the Castle.

She could visualise all too clearly the Prince spiriting the Princess away from Hungary and making sure that she was not only comfortable, but also safe in his beautiful Manor House.

It was not surprising too that the doctor was grateful for what he had done for him.

Then she asked herself how many other people he had helped and was certain that one of them was Thomas.

"I hope he will tell me his story," she thought, "or perhaps the Princess will."

But there was another question to which she longed to know the answer.

119

Who was the 'poor lady'? And if she was living in the house, why had she not seen her?

* * * * *

On Wednesday that which Forella was expecting finally arrived.

It came by Post-Chaise from London, and as soon as she saw what had been brought up to her bedroom she thought it was typical of the Prince's forethought and his eye for detail.

There were two trunks, on each of which was stamped a coronet over the letter 'R'.

When they were unstrapped Mrs Newman and one of the housemaids came to unpack them, and it was then Forella saw the clothes the Prince had bought for her.

"I was beginning to think, M'Lady, that your luggage would never turn up!" Mrs Newman exclaimed when the trunks were open. "It's these transportation difficulties that cause the trouble, despite the fact there are trains running from the coast to London, which should make things easier."

Forella did not speak and she went on:

"Nasty, dirty things they are too. I wouldn't risk my life in one of them!"

Forella did not bother to reply because she was looking at the gowns and thinking they were more attractive and would suit her better than those her aunt had bought.

The Marchioness had been intent on making Forella look sensational so as to catch the eye of some prospective husband.

The Prince, on the other hand, she thought must have used his Hungarian instinct to know what would suit her best, and what in his own words would be a 'suitable frame for her beauty'.

The gowns were comparatively simple, but they had a distinction which she felt made them different from those she had seen on anybody else.

They were not the simple white of an English débutante but were instead the colours of the alpine flowers that filled the steppes after the snows had gone and which her mother had described to her so often.

The soft blues, pinks and golden yellows seemed to have a natural life of their own, and remained unspoilt by the touch of man.

Every gown was original in design and so attractive that Forella longed to see herself at once in each one of them.

She decided first to try on a gown of soft green that seemed to accentuate the green of her eyes and make her skin dazzlingly white.

As Mrs Newman buttoned her into it she said:

"Now you look, M'Lady, like a breath of spring, and it's something you've brought to us ever since you've been at the Manor."

"Thank you, Mrs Newman," Forella replied in surprise.

"It's true, M'Lady. When I hears you laugh and sees you running down the stairs, you makes me feel as if I were young again myself, and that's the truth!"

"You could not say anything kinder or nicer," Forella smiled.

Because she wanted to show the Princess her new gown she hurried along the landing.

Then as she reached the top of the stairs she realised there was somebody outside the front door.

She paused and then as she saw a man walk into the Hall she felt her heart leap.

It was the Prince, who they had been hoping would come to see them.

She was about to call out, but there was no need.

As if what she was feeling drew him, he looked up and smiled when he saw her looking over the banisters.

She started quickly down the stairs and he watched her progress, waiting until she reached the Hall.

Then he put out both his hands to take hers.

"You are all right?" he asked.

"Yes, and so very, very glad to see you!" Forella answered. "The Princess and I thought perhaps you had forgotten us."

"It would be impossible for me to do that," he replied, "and may I say that you are looking very lovely!"

Forella glanced down at her gown.

"It has just arrived, and I am so glad I can show it to you."

"It suits you."

"That is what I thought, and I felt, although I suppose it is an impossibility, that you had chosen it . . . specially for . . . me."

"Shall I say I described what I wanted and what you looked like to somebody who I knew would understand?"

"You are so clever," Forella said, "as well as being so . . . *very kind*!"

The way she said the last words made the Prince say:

"I have a feeling that my cousin has been talking to you!"

"It was very interesting to hear what she told me."

"I might have guessed no woman can keep a secret!" the Prince remarked provocatively as they walked towards the Drawing-Room.

"I have kept mine," Forella said in a low voice, "and please, you must tell me what is happening."

122

"Of course," he answered, "but first I must greet my cousin."

They went into the Drawing-Room and the Princess gave a cry of joy at seeing the Prince.

"János!" she exclaimed. "I was so afraid you would go back to London without coming to see us."

"I had to wait until my last guest had departed," the Prince replied, "and I must say somewhat reluctantly."

"That is what I suspected must have happened," the Princess said. "They impose on you, as we all do."

"That is not true. And even if it is, I like it!"

"Then that is all that matters," the Princess replied.

Then as she looked at Forella for the first time she exclaimed:

"Your clothes have arrived! Oh, I am glad! And what a pretty gown! You look beautiful in it, does she not, János?"

"I have just been telling her so," the Prince replied.

As he spoke his eyes met Forella's and for some reason she could not understand she found it hard to look away.

He had ridden over, as she might have expected, and she thought that in his highly polished boots and cut-away coat he looked so smart and so exceedingly handsome that he might have stepped out of a picture of a Georgian Buck.

Then she knew that, however conventionally dressed he might be, he did not look English.

There was something dashingly foreign about him which she could not put exactly into words.

Newman came hurrying into the Drawing-Room and behind him was one of the footmen carrying a tray on which there was a bottle of champagne in a silver ice-cooler.

"Are we toasting anything special today?" the Princess asked.

"We are celebrating that you look better than I have seen you for some time, Cousin Maria," the Prince answered, "and that Forella looks happy."

"I am happy!" Forella exclaimed.

"And so am I," the Princess interposed. "These last few days I have been more amused by Forella than I have been for years."

"That is what I wanted you to say."

Newman had poured out the champagne and when they each had a glass of it in their hands the Prince raised his.

"To happiness!" he said simply. "What could be a more important toast for us all?"

He drank the champagne in his glass as he spoke, then put it down on a table and said:

"Will you allow me, Cousin Maria, to take Forella out into the garden? I have one or two personal things to discuss with her."

"Yes, of course," the Princess replied, "but be careful she does not spoil her new gown."

"Of course I will be very careful of that," the Prince answered mock-seriously.

They walked through the french windows into the garden, and as they walked over the green lawn Forella said:

"What has happened? You must tell me."

"I can give you the best answer to that," the Prince replied, "by saying 'nothing'!"

"Nothing?"

"I think your uncle was surprised and your aunt very angry when they read your note."

"And the Earl?"

"I imagine your aunt showed it to him, for he certainly seemed more cheerful at the end of the day

124

than he was at the beginning, and he spent every moment with Lady Esme until her husband arrived."

As the Prince finished speaking he realised that Forella was staring at him in sheer astonishment.

"Her . . . husband?" she asked, as if she thought she could not have heard him aright. "Do you mean to . . . say that Lady Esme is . . . married?"

"Of course she is married, I thought you knew!" the Prince said. "Her husband is Sir Richard Meldrum, a very distinguished Diplomat."

"But . . . I had no idea!" Forella exclaimed. "Then if she is married . . . why was she . . . flirting with the Earl? And why did he go to her . . . bedroom?"

The innocence of the question made the Prince draw in his breath. Then he said:

"I think it is a mistake, Forella, for you to be interested in or to worry about those you have left behind for your new life. You and I know the power of thought, and perhaps by thinking of them too much you will attract their attention to yourself."

Forella gave a little cry of horror.

"That is something I do not want . . . and I am sure you are right."

She thought before she continued:

"When we were in India Papa told me that some Indians knew either by thought or instinct when something had happened hundreds of miles away at the very time it was happening."

"That is true," the Prince said, "so I want you to promise me to stop thinking first about your uncle and aunt, and secondly about the Earl. There is no reason for him ever to encroach on your life again."

"Are you saying," Forella asked after a moment, "that I should stay here . . . for ever?"

"No, of course not," the Prince replied. "I have plans for you, although I would rather not talk about them at the moment."

He knew she looked at him curiously and he said:

"I have asked you to trust me."

"I do trust you!" Forella replied. "How can I do anything else when you have been so kind to me? In future I will not only . . . guard my tongue but also my . . . thoughts."

The Prince laughed.

"I am sure that is very sensible," he said, "and the great art of disguise is to think yourself into the part you have to play."

"That is what I am trying to do," Forella said. "The Princess is, I know, convinced that I am Hungarian, and so is everybody else in the house."

"You *are* Hungarian!"

"At the same time I have never been in Hungary, and I am always afraid of making a . . . mistake."

"What has happened to that bright intelligence which you told me was so very precious?" the Prince asked.

"Now you are trying to frighten me," Forella replied. "However, as I have been lucky so far . . . I am sure I shall be . . . in the . . . future."

"I am sure you will," he smiled.

"My luck is all due to you," Forella said in a low voice, "and I shall never, never forget that you saved me when I was . . . alone and frightened . . . from having to go back . . . ignominiously to the Castle and . . . marry the Earl."

"Forget it, forget it all!" the Prince said.

He spoke violently, and Forella said meekly:

"I will try . . . because you have asked me to . . . and I . . . want to please . . . you."

"You do please me," the Prince said, "and I only wish I could stay and see you wearing the other gowns I have chosen for you."

"You . . . you are . . . leaving us?"

It was almost a cry.

"I have to go to London today," the Prince said, "but I will come back as soon as I can."

"Promise me you will do . . . that."

Forella did not know why, but she wanted to hold onto him, she wanted to prevent him from going, she wanted him to stay.

"I promise," the Prince said, "and perhaps next time I shall be able to stay longer."

"You know how much it will mean to the . . . Princess."

Then as if she could not help herself she added:

"And to . . . me!"

The Prince did not respond and she felt there was a strange expression on his face.

As they turned to walk back to the house several doves rose from the bushes just ahead of them and flew away with a flutter of their wings.

"I remember what I wanted to ask you," Forella said. "Both the doctor and Mrs Newman mentioned somebody they both referred to as 'the poor lady'. Who do they mean?"

Even as she spoke she felt she had made a mistake. The Prince was frowning, and there was a grim expression on his face that she had never seen before.

Then when she wanted to say that she was sorry she had been curious and she should not have been so inquisitive, he replied in a voice that had no expression in it whatsoever:

"They were speaking of my wife!"

6

For a moment it was impossible for Forella to speak.

Then in a voice that did not sound like her own she managed to repeat:

"Your . . . wife?"

She had never imagined for one moment, it had simply never crossed her mind that the Princess might be living in the Manor, or even be in England.

And yet now it seemed a reasonable place for the Prince to bring his wife who was obviously an invalid.

They had reached the house, but instead of going in through the french windows, by which they had left it, the Prince suddenly turned round.

Taking Forella by the arm he walked back into the garden across the green lawn, through some shrubs into a part she had visited only once.

It was wilder than the rest of the garden with shrubs rather than flowers, and at the end of it was a small summer house that Forella imagined was seldom used.

The Prince paused, and she saw that just under the thatched roof which was covered with climbing roses there was a wooden seat with cushions on it.

It was part of the perfection that was so evident in everything to do with him that a servant must every day in the summer put the cushions ready on the wooden seat in case anybody should wish to go there.

By now it was impossible to think of anything but what the Prince had just told her, and how surprising it was to be under the same roof as his wife.

They sat down on the seat. Then he said:

"I want to tell you about my wife, Forella, and I would rather do so myself than that you should hear a garbled version from someone else."

Because she felt there was a note of pain in his voice Forella said quickly:

"Please do not tell me . . . if you would . . . rather not. I am sorry if I seemed . . . curious."

"It is understandable.

He did not smile but sat staring in front of him with what Forella felt were unseeing eyes.

Then after what seemed to her to be an uncomfortable pause he began:

"I was married when I was very young to the daughter of a neighbouring landowner whose family was equal in importance to mine. Although the marriage was arranged by my father and the father of the bride, when I saw Gisella, she was so exquisitely beautiful that I fell very much in love with her."

For some reason she did not understand, Forella felt a strange emotion inside her when he spoke of his wife.

Although she did not say anything or move, she knew perceptively he was aware that she was listening intently.

"It was only after we were married, because we had seen very little of each other before," the Prince said, "that I realised Gisella was very, very young for her age, in fact, in many ways completely child-like."

He gave a sigh that seemed to come from the very depths of his being before he went on:

"That is the whole story. Gisella never grew up and although I think her parents must have been aware of her affliction, they were so delighted at the marriage that they said nothing which might have prevented it."

Forella made a little exclamation, but she did not speak and after a moment the Prince continued:

"Only when I understood that Gisella was totally unable to concentrate on anything for more than a few seconds, and that a flower or a butterfly would amuse her while I as a man had really no place in her life, that I faced the truth."

"Was there no . . . chance that she could . . . get better?" Forella managed to ask.

"As you can imagine," the Prince replied, "I took her to every doctor in Hungary, Austria and France, but they merely confirmed what I knew already, that she was a child who would never grow up."

He paused before he continued:

"She had, they told me, suffered brain-damage, perhaps at her birth, perhaps through being dropped as a baby, they could not be sure of the reason."

Now there was a note of pain in the Prince's voice that was unmistakable and as instinctively Forella put out her hand towards him he said in a sharper tone:

"That is not all!"

"What else?"

"As Gisella grew older her temper became uncontrollable and occasionally dangerous."

"Oh . . . no!"

The exclamation of horror seemed to burst from Forella's lips.

"That is why," the Prince went on as if she had not spoken, "she always has to have two nurses with her and cannot be allowed to see anybody else. She may

130

go for a week, perhaps a month or two, without an attack, then when it comes it is frightening."

Again he took a deep breath before he said:

"That is all, but I wanted you to know the truth."

"I am glad . . . you told me," Forella said, "but it . . . hurts me to think what you must have . . . suffered."

"I do not want sympathy," the Prince said in a hard voice. "I have many compensations in life, and I am grateful for them."

She thought he was referring to his horses, his wealth, his position both in Hungary and in England, but now for the first time she realised that beneath all the artificial trappings, the glitter and the glamour, he must be a lonely man.

"In the same way that you have . . . helped so . . . many people," Forella said softly, "I . . . wish I could . . . help you."

For the first time since they had sat down in the summer-house he turned to look at her and now there was an expression in his eyes she did not understand, as he said:

"I am making arrangements to send you away to somewhere where you will be safe. To Hungary, for if your relatives will not welcome you, then mine will!"

"To Hungary?" Forella exclaimed almost beneath her breath. "But . . . it is so far . . . and I should be frightened . . . please . . . can I not stay here? I am so happy with the Princess . . . and I can also . . . sometimes see you."

Her eyes were raised upwards and as the Prince looked down at her she felt as if quite suddenly his grey eyes seemed to grow until everything else vanished and they filled the world, the sky, the whole Universe!

For a second – or a century – time stood still.

Then he said in a tone she had never heard before:

"For God's sake do not make things more difficult than they are already! You have to go! You must be aware why."

Forella gave a little gasp.

Then with a movement almost as violent as the tone of his voice, the Prince rose from the seat and walked away quickly.

He had vanished between the shrubs almost before she could realise what was happening.

Only when he was out of sight and yet his voice seemed still to be ringing on the air did she realise what he had said and knew that she loved him.

*　　*　　*　　*　　*

The Prince drove his horses through Regent's Park, north towards St John's Wood where there were some small attractive houses standing in their own gardens.

He drew up at one of the larger of them and handed the reins to his groom.

"Walk the horses, Higson!" he said. "I shall not be long."

"Very good, Your Highness!"

The Prince stepped down and raised the silver knocker on the door.

It was opened after a short wait by a maid-servant wearing a lace-edged apron and a starched white cap also trimmed with lace.

She looked surprised at seeing him and bobbed a curtsy.

"Good morning, Your Highness! *Ma'mselle*'s not expecting you."

"I know that," the Prince replied entering the small hall.

He put down his top-hat and gloves and the maid

waiting at the foot of the stairs asked:

"Will Your Highness go up to *Ma'mselle*, or shall I tell her you're here?"

The Prince paused for a moment before he replied:

"Tell *Mademoiselle* that I wish to speak to her in the Sitting-Room."

"Very good, Your Highness."

The Prince walked into the Sitting-Room which was beautifully furnished and had windows over-looking both the front and the back of the house.

Besides the flowers in vases, and there was a profusion of them, there were also huge baskets of orchids.

One of them of purple cattleya completely filled the fireplace, another on a table by the window partially obscured the view of the garden.

The Prince put down on a small side table two things he had carried in. Then he stood still in a way that was not quite natural, and there was an expression on his face that Forella would have known perceptively was one of pain.

It was nearly five minutes before there was the sound of feet running swiftly down the stairs and the door opened and Lucille de Pre came into the room.

The grace of her body and the manner in which she moved would have told any observer who was not aware of her fame that she was a ballerina.

She was also beautiful with almost perfect features and huge eyes that were accentuated by the mascara on her long eyelashes.

She was wearing only a *negligee* over her night-gown, and her dark hair which reached below her waist was tied back with pink satin ribbon.

"*Mon cher*, what a surprise!" she exclaimed in French and held out her arms to the Prince.

However, he prevented her from coming any nearer

to him by taking both her hands in his and kissing them one after the other.

"I did not expect you so early," Lucille said, "and actually, I am angry with you because you have not been to see me for what seems a very long time."

"I have, however, heard of your triumph," the Prince replied.

"It is *fantastique*, is it not? The newspapers have written about me, and the Director has gone on his knees to beg me to extend my contract."

She spoke with an elation and a lilt in her voice which told him how much it meant to her.

"I am glad, so very glad," the Prince said, "and I have brought you a present."

"I should thank you for the flowers, and for the present you sent me on the first night."

"This is a different present."

He turned to the side table and picking up the square velvet-covered box he opened it.

Lucille gave a gasp.

Inside in the centre of the box was a diamond necklace which glittered against a black velvet background, and there were two drop ear-rings and a wide bracelet to match.

"*C'est magnifique!*" Lucille cried. "How can I tell you how thrilled I am to possess anything so fabulous!"

Again she held out her arms but the Prince avoided them and picked up the other thing he had placed on the side table.

This consisted of some sheets of parchment tied with red tape, which the Prince handed to Lucille saying:

"My other present is the deeds of this house."

She stared at him, but she did not speak, and he went on:

134

"I have also deposited a sum of money in your Bank which will keep you in comfort for a very long time, even if you are not earning the astronomical fees you are getting now."

Lucille was still. Then she looked up at him to ask:

"Why are you giving me all these things?"

"They are to thank you for the happiness we have found together."

"For three years?" she murmured.

"As you say, for three years."

There was silence. Then Lucille asked:

"Are you saying that you are leaving me?"

"We both agreed," the Prince said quietly, "that if at any time either of us wished to break what was a very close and very perfect friendship, then we would part without explanations or recriminations."

"I know we said that," Lucille replied, "but I did not think – I never imagined – "

She stopped. Then she said:

"What you are telling me is that there is – somebody else."

"There is, but I have no wish to speak of it," the Prince replied. "I only want to wish you great happiness, Lucille, which I know you will find, and of course continued success and the acclaim which has already reverberated throughout London."

Lucille did not answer. She only stared down at the jewels in the box which she held in her hands.

The Prince put the deeds back on the table from where he had taken them. Then he looked at her for a long moment before he said very quietly:

"Goodbye, Lucille, and thank you."

Only as she heard the door shut behind him did she seem to come out of the trance which had held her silent.

"Wait! Wait!" she cried.

She ran across the room to pull open the door he had closed.

But already he had gone from the house.

As she reached the front door he was driving away and she only had a glimpse of his back disappearing down the road.

It was then she flung the jewel-box and its contents down on the floor, and burst into tears.

*　　*　　*　　*　　*

"I wonder when János will come and see us again?" the Princess said as Forella shut the book she had been reading aloud.

She knew as the Princess spoke that she had not really been listening, and if she was honest that her mind too had been on other things, or rather on one thing.

She had found it impossible ever since the Prince had gone to think of anything but him.

She had found when she finally returned to the Manor that he had already left and the Princess was grumbling that his visit had been so short.

"Now we may not see him for weeks," she said, "but I suppose I must not complain. It is only through his kindness that I am safe here."

"I suppose he is . . . going to . . . London," Forella said, finding it hard to speak.

"Of course," the Princess replied, "and that means his social friends, including the Prince and Princess of Wales, will be waiting there for him eagerly, just as we are."

When she went to bed that night, Forella had lain awake thinking of the Prince and knowing her love for him had increased until she felt with every beat of her heart that she loved him more.

She told herself it was ridiculous, absurd, something she should not have allowed to happen.

But she knew that just as she was perceptive about other things, her instinct had drawn her to the Prince from the very first moment she saw him.

While her mind had tried to decry him as being part of the Social World which she disliked and mistrusted, her heart had told her even then that he was very different.

She had fought against the magnetism of him and the fact that he was the most handsome man she had ever seen.

But even before she was told of his exceptional kindness, sympathy and understanding by the people who trusted him, she had known that after he brought her to the Manor, she had been waiting like the Princess eagerly and excitedly to see him again.

Today when she had gone into the hall her heart had turned several somersaults at the sight of him.

She knew that if she had been truthful she would have admitted then that what she was feeling was love, and although he had not said it in so many words, she knew as if it was written in letters of fire that he loved her.

"How is it possible?" her brain argued. "I must have been mistaken."

But when his grey eyes looked into hers and he told her he was sending her away, she knew that the reason was quite simple: it was love.

Forella, however, did not deceive herself for one moment that there could ever be a happy ending to their story.

In the first place the Prince was married; secondly, even if he were free, what could she offer Prince János Kovác with his wealth, his power, his possessions, and most of all himself?

'I am just a nobody, ignorant of his world and

anything in which he is interested, except horses,' she thought. 'When he sends me to Hungary he will . . . forget about me . . . while I will . . . never forget . . . him.'

Moreover she had to suppose that the Prince's affection for her must be only a transitory one when the Princess told her of his success in London, Paris and everywhere else in the world.

"He is admired and respected," the Princess said, "not only by the statesmen and sportsmen of each country, but also by their beautiful women."

Because the Princess had little to think about at the moment except for her cousin who had saved her from imprisonment and perhaps death, she pored over the Social Columns of the newspapers to find out what Prince János was doing, whom he was entertaining, and who was entertaining him.

She cut every mention of his name out of the newspapers.

There was one drawer, Forella discovered, in the Drawing-Room which was already half filled with press-cuttings, articles from magazines, and sketches made by artists of the Castle and of the Prince himself.

He would more often than not be sketched leading in the winner of some famous horse-race in which he had won the cup and the prize money against competitors from the most famous stables in the country.

Because it was a bitter-sweet pleasure to talk about him, Forella encouraged the Princess to show her the newspaper reports and assisted her in finding others.

"Listen to this," the Princess had said triumphantly today after the newspapers had arrived which she had immediately opened at the Court Circular.

She read aloud:

"At the Duchess of Manchester's Ball last night the Princess of Wales, looking radiantly beautiful in grey silk trimmed with Venetian lace, was talking to handsome Prince János Kovác.

Later the Prince, one of the most successful race-horse owners in Europe as well as in England, took in to supper the lovely Marchioness of Sheen whose exquisite face has been immortalised in no less than three portraits to be exhibited in the Royal Academy this year."

The Princess put down the newspaper for a moment.

"The Marchioness of Sheen," she said reflectively. "That is a new beauty, and I am prepared to wager quite a large sum of money that she will soon be a guest at the Castle."

"Does His Highness invite . . . only beautiful . . . women to . . . stay with him?" Forella asked in a low voice.

"But of course!" the Princess replied. "Why should he entertain plain ones? More than any other man, János expects perfection."

She gave a little laugh.

"In his horses, in his houses, and of course in his women!"

"*His* women!"

The words seemed to echo in Forella's mind and repeat and repeat themselves all through the night.

The days which before had been a sheer delight now seemed to pass slowly, while the nights seemed interminable.

Everywhere she looked, everything she heard, everything she thought seemed to be part of the Prince.

"He has taken possession of me," she told herself.

While in a way it was a frightening thought,

something alive and thrilling seemed to leap like a little flame within her almost as if he was touching her.

The days passed without his coming again to the Manor, and her elation began to die away.

The newspapers' reports of the Balls he attended, the Receptions at which he had been present, told her how unimportant and insignificant she was in comparison and that the Prince had forgotten her.

Perhaps he would remember her again when he received an answer from Hungary, and then she would just find herself being sent there.

She would at least be safe from being taken back by her uncle and aunt and forced to marry the Earl of Sherburn. But she would also be exiled from the Prince, the only person now who meant anything in her life.

"How can I . . . leave him . . . how can I . . . lose him?" she asked despairingly.

Yet she knew that when he ordered her to go she would leave, and that would be the end.

As he had not told her that she must not mention his wife to the Princess, after three days of keeping the secret to herself Forella said tentatively:

"When His Highness was . . . here I asked him who was referred to as the . . . 'poor lady', and he told me it was . . . his wife."

The Princess gave a little sigh of relief.

"I am glad he told you," she replied. "I did not like to tell you myself, for fear it would annoy him, but because she is hidden here I knew I should be safe from being sent back to Hungary and from those who wish to hurt me because they hated my husband."

She gave a little laugh before she added:

"Trust János to find the perfect hiding place for all sorts and conditions of people, like the doctor,

Thomas, myself and of course poor Gisella."

"Did you know her?" Forella asked.

"I had never actually spoken to her," the Princess replied, "because I had left home a long time before János married her, but I had seen her in the distance and thought her very beautiful, and a very suitable bride for János – until I learned the truth."

She did not wait for Forella to reply but went on:

"Oh, my poor dear János! How can this have happened to him of all people? I pray every night of my life that one day he will be free and have the family he has always wanted."

Her voice was very moving as she said:

"He needs sons to inherit his title and his vast possessions, and daughters whom I know he would love and who would inevitably be beautiful, because he surrounds himself with nothing but beauty."

"It seems . . . cruel that . . . nothing can be . . . done," Forella faltered.

"Nothing at all!" the Princess agreed. "They are tied 'until death them do part', and Dr Bouvais informs me that the Princess may live for very much longer than János himself!"

Forella wanted to cry out at the injustice of it, but she was afraid of betraying herself to the Princess who she knew had no idea of her feelings for the Prince.

"Do you ever . . . visit the 'poor lady'?" she asked tentatively.

"No," the Princess replied. "János has asked me not to do so, as visitors could excite her, which is a mistake."

"She has her doves?"

"Yes, her doves, although there are now far too many of them!" the Princess replied sharply. "It is not safe for her to have any other animals, but doves can fly away."

There was no need for the Princess to say any more, for the Prince had already told her that his wife was violent at times.

But Forella felt she was vividly conscious of the presence of the 'poor lady' in the other part of the house, and she understood now why there were so many servants.

Now she knew why they never spoke except inadvertantly, of the 'poor lady' who was shut away with her nurses.

'It is a cruel fate for her, and even more cruel for him,' Forella thought.

Although she prayed for them both, as the days passed and the Prince did not come to the Manor, her prayers became more and more despairing.

Then one morning when she was helping her dress Mrs Newman said:

"Now don't you go wandering too far from the house, M'Lady. I saw you yesterday from the windows walking up towards the wood."

"There is a lovely view from there," Forella replied.

"Well, it would be best if you kept to the garden."

"Why?"

There was silence. Then Forella, feeling something was wrong, asked quickly:

"Why should you ask me to do that? What has happened?"

"Perhaps I shouldn't mention it, M'Lady," Mrs Newman replied, "but there's been a man snooping about the place. Thomas sees him hanging about the stables and asks him what he's doing. He said he was just a visitor who had lost his way."

Forella felt her heart give a beat.

Despite the Prince's optimism she had always felt that sooner or later when she did not return her uncle would begin to grow impatient and feel that as he was responsible he must find her.

She had been so intent on thinking about the Prince and so happy and relaxed in the quiet and peace of the Manor that she now felt despairingly that she had been over-confident.

She was not safe, of course she was not safe, since her uncle, who was a very conscientious man, would feel it his duty to find her.

Then she would be taken back to London, Aunt Kathie would immediately announce her engagement to the Earl of Sherburn and she would never be able to run away again.

'What can I do? What can I do?' she thought frantically.

She would have liked to discuss it with the Princess, but thought it might upset her.

Anyway, how could she help, tied as she was to her chair, and powerless when it came to a question of the law?

The Prince would be powerless too because, as Forella was aware, a Guardian had complete and absolute power over his Ward.

If her uncle and aunt were still intent on her marrying the Earl, she would be married to him however much she might protest, or however much he might dislike the idea.

Now in the face of danger she realised the Prince was right in making arrangements for her to go to Hungary.

Once she was out of the country no detective would be able to find her, so the sooner she left the better.

But in the meantime there was always the chance it might be too late.

Before she went out through the front door where she knew Thomas would be waiting for her with Győrgy she ran into the Library and quickly wrote a letter to the Prince.

"*Your Highness,*

There is a man hanging around the house asking questions. He is making everybody nervous, and I am sure it is somebody Uncle George has sent to look for me.

Please come as soon as you can and tell me what I can do. I am frightened, very frightened, and I feel that only you can save me.

Forella."

She placed the note in an envelope, addressed it to the Prince, at his London house, and went out into the Hall where Newman was waiting for her to leave.

"Will you have this posted immediately to the Prince?" she asked.

Then she paused.

"I think it would be . . . quicker if . . . somebody took it to London. It will only take about two-and-a-half hours, and I think the Prince should have it at once."

Newman's impassive face expressed no surprise at the request.

"Yes, of course, M'Lady," he replied. "I will arrange for one of the grooms to leave immediately."

"Thank you," Forella said and hurried outside to where Györgÿ was waiting.

As she rode away on him with Thomas on another magnificent stallion belonging to the Prince she said:

"I have heard that a man has been asking questions around here? Have you seen him? What is he like?"

"I have seen him," Thomas replied, "but he has not spoken to me. I gather, although I may be mistaken, that he is not interested in the stables, for which I am extremely thankful, but in the house."

Forella felt her heart miss a beat before she said:

"You have no idea who he is looking for?"

"None, M'Lady," Thomas replied, "and he may of course be just a Nosey-Parker, or perhaps a burglar 'casing the joint', as they say."

"I feel that a burglar would not ask questions and risk people noticing him," Forella said tentatively.

"No, I'm sure you are right, M'Lady."

He was frowning, however, and Forella said impulsively:

"I expect you are aware that practically everybody here seems to be hiding from something and so it concerns us all."

"That's right," Thomas agreed, "and I have no wish to be recognised."

"I thought . . . perhaps you were . . . hiding, as I am," Forella said.

"Yes, I am hiding," Thomas replied, "and it is thanks entirely to His Highness that I am a free man."

Because they were talking Györgÿ began to shy at anything he noticed, and Forella had to keep a tight rein on him.

"We'll let the horses have their heads, M'Lady," Thomas said, "and talk later. I think they're jealous because we are not attending to them."

Forella laughed and let Györgÿ gallop until she thought he had worked off some of his freshness.

Then when they were able to speak again Thomas told her that he had been a trainer at Newmarket to a very distinguished member of the Jockey Club.

One of his jockeys, desperately anxious to win the 2000 Guineas, had, although Thomas was completely unaware of it, doped the horse he was riding.

He had won the race but another jockey, jealous of his success, had complained to the Stewards who had instituted an enquiry.

The jockey, to save his own face, had sworn that he was innocent and that it was Thomas, the trainer of the horse, who had actually doped the animal to make him go faster.

"It was one of those complicated cases," Thomas said dryly, "and the verdict simply rested on whose word the Stewards believed."

"And they did not believe you!" Forella exclaimed.

"His Highness told me that it was because I had been somewhat revolutionary in my methods of training, and had in the past made several enemies through no fault of my own among other trainers, that they favoured the jockey."

He sighed and added in a low voice:

"There was every chance of my being humiliated and struck off the register."

"That would have been grossly unfair!" Forella cried.

"What happens on a race-course often is," Thomas said philosophically. "His Highness persuaded me that the best thing I could do was not to face the enquiry, but resign from the position I held."

His voice deepened as he went on:

"He helped me to write a letter protesting my innocence but making it clear that I thought it best from the point of view of racing as a great sport that there should be no scandal."

He gave a dry laugh.

"It was a clever letter, and I understand my action was very much approved by the Jockey Club in general."

"So you came here," Forella said.

"Yes, His Highness brought me here and gave me some magnificent horses to look after, which has made life very much pleasanter for me than it might have been otherwise."

"And what of the future?" Forella asked.

Thomas smiled and she realised it was something

146

he seldom did.

"His Highness has promised me that when everything has quietened down and there is no question of
my being recognised, he will set me up as a trainer in
Paris where he has a large stable which he intends to
make larger still."

Forella gave an exclamation of delight.

"That will be splendid for you!"

"I am looking forward to it, M'Lady, but His
Highness insists on my waiting for at least five years
until I am forgotten at Newmarket and there is no
possible way that in France I should be connected
with a trainer whose method of racing was queried by
the Jockey Club."

"I understand."

She thought how right the Princess had been in
describing everybody at the Manor as the Prince's
'lame ducks.'

Because they all had something to hide it was
obvious that anybody asking questions and snooping
about the place would make them nervous and
anxious.

At the same time she was absolutely convinced
that as they had not been spied on before it must be
she who was responsible.

It was the search for her which had brought the
man who was making it difficult for Forella, the
Princess, the doctor, and for all she knew a number of
other people to sleep quietly at night.

'The Prince will settle everything when he comes,'
she thought.

She found herself thinking all the time how long it
would be before the groom reached the house in
London, what the Prince would do when he read her
note, and how soon he would arrive at the Manor.

It was ten days now since she had seen him, but she

thought that to her it seemed like ten centuries.

She had the feeling he was avoiding her, and she kept remembering he had said she was making things worse than they were already. But what exactly did he mean by that?

Perhaps she had read into it something quite different from what he had intended.

Forella suddenly felt very young, very insecure and very ignorant.

After the strange life she had lived with her father and mother, what did she know of men like Prince János? And what, for that matter, did she know of England?

She had met Sultans and Chieftains, Arab Sheiks and men who lived only to fight, to plunder and to kill.

And yet, until she came to England, she had never met men like her uncle or the Earl, and certainly never one like the Prince.

It had been difficult at first to think they were real and not just elegantly dressed characters from a story.

But now, when she thought of the Prince, he was very real. She knew that just to be with him was a joy and a rapture that it was impossible to express in words because it was something which had never happened to her before.

Then she laughed at herself for being so foolish as to think she could ever mean anything to him personally.

She was just another of his 'lame ducks' to whom he had extended his patronage and his compassion.

"He is sorry for me, he pities me. To him I am not an attractive woman like the beautiful ladies who fill his house in London and his Castle, and who amuse him as I am quite unable to do."

At night she thought over every conversation she

had had with the Prince and decided she had been stupid to argue and undoubtedly bore him with her tirades against Society.

To him they must have seemed extremely revolutionary and presumptuous ideas on the part of a young girl.

'I should have just kept quiet and let him do the talking,' she chided herself.

She longed in despair, as many other women had done before her, to put back the clock, and be different from what she had been.

It was impossible to sleep until the stars were fading and there was only an hour before dawn.

Then at last she did slip away into unconsciousness, and she dreamt that the Prince was there and that everything had changed. They were walking together, hand in hand, and she was no longer afraid.

She awoke with a start, and because she felt restless got out of bed and pulled back the curtains.

Her bedroom looked out onto the garden and in the dawn light there was a faint mist over the stream, and everything had that soft translucent quality and the stillness that came just before the dawn.

Then as Forella stood there looking out and thinking, still enraptured by her dream, she looked down.

In the shadows of the bushes which bordered part of the lawn there was something which seemed darker and more bulky than the slender boughs, the leaves and the blossom.

It was difficult to see clearly, until as she stared and something made her go on staring, she was aware that it was a man!

A man – and she was sure he was looking up at the windows of the house.

Although she could not see his face she thought it was her window that he was staring at.

Because she was frightened, although it was unlikely he could see her, she stepped farther back into the room.

Only as she did so did she realise she was trembling.

She was now absolutely certain that whoever her uncle had employed to seek her out had discovered she was at the Manor and disguised under a false name.

7

Walking back from the garden with some roses which she had picked for the Princess, Forella was thinking excitedly that the Prince might come today.

She was sure he would not ignore her appeal, but she was afraid he might not be in London, perhaps watching his horses win on some distant race-course.

But because there was a chance of seeing him she had put on one of the prettiest gowns he had sent her.

She knew as she looked in the mirror that her eyes were bright with excitement and an expression that made her shy because it was so unmistakably one of love.

It seemed impossible that she should love him so completely and so unexpectedly when she knew so little about him.

But her father had fallen in love with her mother the moment he saw her and her mother had felt the same about him.

"I thought he was the handsomest man I had ever seen," her mother told her. "Then when he looked at me I felt as if my heart leaped out towards him and although even now, it still seems impossible, I fell in love!"

"I understand," Forella told herself, "and just as Mama loved Papa all her life, so will I never be able to love anybody else in the same way as I love Prince János."

Then she remembered the 'poor lady' upstairs and felt as if there was a shadow over the sun.

At the moment the one thing that was more important than anything else was the possibility that she had been traced.

Unless the Prince could save her again she would be taken back to London, and after being scolded severely by her aunt, she would be made to marry the Earl whether she wished it or not.

'If the Prince does not come by tomorrow, then perhaps I had better run away,' Forella thought.

But now after the security and happiness of being at the Manor she could no longer contemplate, as she had done before, setting off on her own on György without knowing where she was going and with very little money.

"The Prince will come, I know he will come to me!" she told herself consolingly.

Then as she walked through the french windows into the Drawing-Room he was there!

She had not expected him so early and for the moment she thought he had just stepped out of her dreams.

But he was real, he was human, and he was standing looking at her with an expression in his eyes that made it impossible to breathe.

She had no idea that because she had her back to the sun the red lights in her hair were dancing like little tongues of flame and she looked exceedingly lovely.

After what seemed a very long time Forella managed to murmur:

"You . . . are here!"

Her voice broke the spell between them and the

Prince walked forward.

"Yes, I am here," he said in his deep voice. "I came as soon as I could."

"It is . . . so early," Forella said, "that the Princess will . . . not be ready to . . . see you."

She was not thinking of what she was saying.

She was only aware of how handsome he was, and his nearness made her feel that shafts of sunshine were piercing her body and becoming, as they touched her heart, little flames of fire.

"It is you I want to see," the Prince said quietly. "But first, I want to find out exactly what has been happening here, and what is the reason for it."

As he finished speaking, to Forella's surprise a young boy came running into the room.

"I have found them, Uncle János!" he cried excitedly, "and now I want to use them."

The Prince smiled and said:

"Miklos, let me first present you to a very charming lady. Forella, this is my nephew and he has come to England to go to school where he will in future be known as 'Michael'."

Forella held out her hand and Miklos, who was about twelve years old, bowed over it in the most elegant manner before he said as if he wanted her to join in his excitement:

"Do you know what I have here?"

He was carrying a box in his hand and Forella answered:

"I have no idea."

"Uncle János tells me it is a telescope that was used at the Battle of Trafalgar, and as I am going to be a sailor when I grow up I want to know how to use one myself."

"Actually," the Prince said, "there are two telescopes in the box, and I think you might show the

Countess how to use one."

"Of course," Miklos agreed.

The Prince looked at Forella.

"Take Miklos into the garden," he said, "and when I have seen Thomas for whom I have sent, I will know more and we can talk about it."

Forella put the roses she was carrying down on a side table and as she did so Miklos ran ahead out of the french windows and into the garden.

"Do not be frightened," the Prince said in a low voice. "You know I will look after you."

"I saw the man last night . . . looking up at . . . my window," Forella answered. "I am sure Uncle George . . . must have sent him to . . . find me."

"Trust me," the Prince said, "and perhaps it is not as dangerous as you fear."

"I hope . . . not."

She wanted to stay with him, she wanted to go on talking just so that she could be near him.

Then there was a knock on the door and she knew it must be Thomas. Without saying any more, she went quickly through the window into the garden in search of Miklos.

When she joined him she said:

"You must tell me all about the history of the telescopes."

"Uncle János says they are very precious and also at the time they were the strongest telescopes that had ever been made."

He opened the box, and Forella looking down saw two telescopes lying side by side.

"I think," she said, "if we go towards the wood there is a good view from there, and we can find out how far we can see with them."

"Yes, please let us do that," Miklos agreed.

He was a good-looking little boy and Forella

thought as she had before how cruel it was that the Prince could not have a son of his own.

She was quite certain if he did have one the boy would be very handsome.

The Prince would want to teach him to ride as well as he did, and to take part in all the other pursuits at which she was certain he was very proficient.

She thought it must be a poor substitute for him to interest himself in his sister's children, and she had learnt from the Princess that he had no brothers.

"Where are you going to school?" she asked Miklos.

"Uncle János has arranged for me to go to Eton," he answered. "He says it is the best school in the world, and I am very fortunate. But first I am going to a crammer."

"I am sure you will enjoy Eton as much as my father did," Forella replied.

By this time they had reached the steps at the end of the garden which led up into the wood.

When they had climbed a little way Forella thought it would be wiser for them not to go any further, just in case they encountered the man who had been watching the house.

She therefore stopped and said:

"Let us discover how far we can see from here."

Miklos was only too willing.

He put the box down on the ground, took out the two telescopes and handed one to her.

"I expect you know how to adjust it," he said.

"I think so," Forella smiled.

She took it from him and looked out over the valley to realise that there was a heat haze which made it difficult to see very clearly.

She swung the telescope round towards the house, wishing as she did so that she could see the Prince.

Then she had an idea.

"I tell you what we will do, Miklos," she said. "If we both look through the telescopes we can see the white doves on the roof and the gables and the windows. We will have a competition to see who can count the most."

"I like that," Miklos exclaimed, "and what will be the prize?"

"You will have to ask your Uncle János that," Forella replied. "Tell me when you are ready to start."

"I am ready now!"

"Very well," Forella replied, putting the telescope to her right eye and shutting the other one. "One – two – three – Go!"

The telescopes were quite strong, and she could see the white doves very clearly fluttering around the gables.

Then she realised there was a number of them on one of the window-sills on the third floor and knew it must be where the 'poor lady' fed them.

Without really thinking she began to count the ones that were obviously pecking at something on the sill.

Then as she did so somebody came to the window.

It was a woman. Forella could see her face quite clearly and knew she was looking at the Prince's wife.

There was no doubt that she was still pretty, but it was a child's face and even at such a distance Forella thought she looked very, very young.

Then as she stared at her, forgetting for the moment about the doves, there was suddenly a flutter of wings and she was aware that the Princess was leaning a long way out of the window.

It passed through Forella's mind that it was dangerous and she might fall.

Even as she thought it she saw the 'poor lady's'

hands reaching out into space as if she was trying to save herself, and realised with a feeling of horror that she was not falling but being pushed!

There was a man behind her, and she could see his arms and his shoulders.

Then as the 'poor lady' fell from the window into space Forella felt she could almost hear the scream that must have come from her lips.

It was all so quick, there was a flutter of white that was like the wings of the doves, then the 'poor lady' had vanished.

It seemed impossible that it had happened!

Then as Forella still looked there was a man in the window and she could see his face quite clearly.

It was somebody she had never seen before with dark hair and a heavy black moustache.

He looked down at the ground, then moved back and disappeared inside.

As Forella gasped at what she had seen Miklos beside her exclaimed:

"Somebody fell out of the window! Did you see? She fell! I saw her!"

"That . . . is what I . . . thought."

"And there was a man at the window. Why did he not save her?"

"Perhaps it was . . . impossible to do . . . so."

Then because what she had seen was so frightening and at the same time it seemed as if it could not really have happened and had just been a trick of the telescope, she said:

"I . . . I think, Miklos, we should . . . go back to the house."

"We must go and tell Uncle János what we have seen," Miklos replied. "Do you think the lady who fell has been hurt?"

"I do not . . . know," Forella answered, "but we

must . . . find out."

Her words were almost incoherent.

Then it was impossible to say any more because they had reached the lawn and she started to run.

Miklos ran beside her, grasping his telescope and the box which he had remembered to pick up.

Only as they drew nearer to the house did Forella go a little slower so as to catch her breath.

She wanted to reach the Prince, at the same time she was afraid the whole thing had been some strange illusion.

Yet she knew she had actually seen it happen, and so had Miklos.

They reached the Drawing-Room window and Miklos was just about to run ahead and tell his uncle what he had seen, when Forella heard voices and put her hand out to hold onto him.

"Wait a moment," she whispered.

She did not want to tell the Prince what had happened in the presence of somebody else.

Then as she stood irresolutely, wondering how she could break the news to him of what had occurred, she heard him say angrily in a voice she did not recognise:

"What are you saying, Jacques? And you have not yet explained why you are here."

He was speaking in French, and as Forella wondered who the stranger could be a man answered:

"You have exactly two minutes, Kovác, to make up your mind what you will do. The choice is yours!"

"What the devil are you talking about?"

"I will make it very clear – Lucille and I came here together."

"Lucille is here?"

"Listen, you have no time to talk. She told the nurse attending your wife that she had sprained her ankle, and while they were out of the room somebody pushed that poor, crazy creature out of the window!"

"I have not the slightest idea what you are saying!" the Prince exclaimed.

"The choice," Jacques went on as if he had not spoken, "is whether you swear that you will marry my sister, or else be accused of murder! I am prepared to state that I saw you throw your wife out of the window when there was nobody else in the room."

"I think you are either mad or drunk!" the Prince said angrily. "My head groom was with me until one second before you came into the room."

"Your servant's evidence would not be admissible in a Court of Law when it comes to a case of murder," Jacques said scornfully. "So which is it to be, Kovác – marriage or a trial at the Old Bailey?"

It was then Forella drew a deep breath and, taking Miklos by the hand, walked with him through the open window into the Drawing-Room.

She had realised while the Prince was talking to the Frenchman called Jacques that the small boy did not understand French.

As they came into the Drawing-Room together she saw as she expected that the man standing facing the Prince had a heavy black moustache and was the man she had seen at the window.

The Prince looked up as they appeared, and before Forella could say anything Miklos ran to his uncle's side.

"Uncle János," he cried, "I looked through the telescope and I saw a lady in white fall out of a window! I saw her!"

"You have one minute more," the Frenchman said, as if he wished to push aside the interruption.

"I also saw what happened," Forella said in French. "The 'poor lady' fell from the window, but she was pushed by a man who looked out afterwards to see where she had fallen."

She paused before she made a gesture with her hand towards the Frenchman and said:

"That was the man I saw!"

Jacques started, then he said furiously:

"More servants' evidence? I doubt if it would carry any weight before a judge and jury!"

"My name, *Monsieur*, if you are interested," Forella said slowly in French, "is Forella Claye, and my uncle is the Marquess of Claydon who is Lord-in-Waiting to Her Majesty Queen Victoria!"

She spoke clearly and positively and it was almost as if she watched the Frenchman crumble before her eyes.

He knew he was defeated and although he wanted to bluster further his eyes shifted and he seemed suddenly to grow smaller as the Prince said in a voice of authority:

"There is now one minute for you and Lucille to get out of this house and then out of the country! If you remain in the vicinity, you will be apprehended on a charge of murder, and my guest who saw what happened will give evidence which means that you will be hanged!"

Jacques opened his lips to speak and the Prince said in a voice of thunder:

"One minute!"

Then almost as quickly as the 'poor lady' had fallen Jacques had run from the room, slamming the door behind him.

Because she had been so tense and at the same time so afraid for the Prince, Forella felt as if the walls were moving round her and there was a darkness coming up from the floor.

But the Prince's arms supported her and he helped

160

her to a sofa as Miklos was asking:

"Why did that man run away? I saw him in the window after the lady fell."

The Prince took his arms from Forella.

"Miklos," he said quietly, "I want you to do something for me."

"What is it, Uncle János?"

"I want you to go to the stables to look at the horses, and take the Countess with you."

"I would like to do that, Uncle János."

"You are to say nothing – do you understand? – nothing of what you have seen or heard until you have talked to me about it. It is very important, and I know you will do as I tell you."

"Yes, of course, Uncle János."

The Prince turned again to Forella.

"Are you all right?" he asked. "If so, I would like you to leave this room as quickly as you can."

"I . . . I am all . . . right," Forella replied in a whisper.

"You have saved me," the Prince said, "and now I want to save you and everybody else from a great deal of unpleasantness."

Forella rose to her feet.

The weakness had passed, and she really did feel all right. It was because the Prince was near her, he had touched her and she loved him.

She put out her hand to Miklos.

"Come along," she said, "I know you will enjoy seeing your uncle's horses."

The Prince walked to the door and opened it for them.

"Thank you," he said very softly, as Forella passed him and the words were like a caress.

The Hall was empty.

Then as Forella and Miklos turned left down the

corridor which led them to the side door that was nearest to the stables, she saw Newman coming from the opposite direction.

He was moving very much more quickly than he usually did and she heard him say breathlessly as he reached the Prince:

"I must ask Your Highness to come at once! There has been a terrible accident!"

*   *   *   *   *

Afterwards Forella found it difficult to remember exactly what had happened and in what order everything had taken place, for it had all been so dramatic as to seem unreal.

It did not seem possible that the 'poor lady' was dead and the Prince was free.

While she was in the stables with Miklos feeding the horses and pretending to listen while Thomas explained to the small boy how they had been bred and where they had come from, all she could think of was the Prince.

Perhaps after all his wife had suffered only from shock and had not been murdered as the Frenchman had intended.

She wondered vaguely who he was and who 'Lucille' might be, and also why the Prince should be blackmailed into marrying her.

Then she thought that it was only justice that, as he had saved her from being married to the Earl, so she had saved him from being forced into marrying somebody who must have conspired with her brother to murder the 'poor lady'.

It all seemed so complicated and so horrible, and yet she could not help a little flicker of irrepressible happiness at the idea that if the 'poor lady' was dead the Prince was a free man.

'Even if he does not . . . want me,' she thought, 'since I love him . . . I want his . . . happiness.'

Thomas lifted Miklos onto the back of one of the magnificent stallions.

"I want to ride this horse," Miklos said. "Do you think Uncle János will let me?"

"You will have to ask His Highness yourself," Thomas answered.

"There is no time today," Miklos said, "because Mama is waiting at the Castle to take me to a crammer."

"Perhaps next holidays," Thomas said with a smile.

"Yes, of course, next holidays," Miklos agreed.

Forella was wondering where she would be when the holidays came round and if she would be in Hungary from where Miklos had just come.

Her mind seemed to be going round and round in circles and she kept seeing the out-stretched arms of the 'poor lady' as she tried to find something to hold on to as Jacques pushed her from the window.

Now she could think about it clearly she knew that the Prince in telling him to get out of the house and out of the country was not seeking to save him from the consequences of his crime, but to avoid the scandal and the publicity which would ensue from a murder trial.

It was not only something he would shrink from and dislike above everything, but so many other people would suffer like the Princess, the doctor, Thomas and herself.

If the Police were brought in and it was a question of a trial, they would all be expected to give evidence and their anonymity would be swept away.

'Then Uncle George would know where I was without even having to look for me,' Forella thought in horror.

She realised that last night when she had seen Jacques looking, as she thought, at her window, he had been actually looking up at the window where the 'poor lady' slept.

She was certain now he had been trying to find out for the last few days, when he had been snooping about and questioning the servants, exactly how the household was organised.

He would have learnt that while one nurse was having her luncheon the other would be on duty alone. That was why Lucille, whoever she might be, had asked her to attend to her sprained ankle.

Jacques had thus made sure there was nobody with the 'poor lady' when he entered the room and she was feeding her doves.

Watching her as he must have done, he would have been aware that the doves were always greedy for anything she could give them, and it had been easy for him because she was small to tip her out of the window as Forella and Miklos had seen him do.

'It was a chance in a million!' Forella thought, 'That we should have been watching through the telescopes.'

And yet perhaps it was a Power greater than chance that ensured the Prince should not be accused of a wicked deed that he would never in the nobility of his heart have contemplated.

It was as if her prayers had been answered directly, and as she prayed for his happiness God had listened and come to the rescue of them both.

"If only . . . that could be . . . true,' Forella whispered to herself and was afraid that perhaps she was being too optimistic.

Then when they had just finished inspecting the horses, one of the footmen came to the stables to say that His Highness wished them to return to the house where he was waiting for them in the Drawing-Room.

Nervous and afraid that something had happened that she did not anticipate, Forella was very pale as they went into the room.

The Prince was standing with his back to the fireplace, and as they came in he said:

"Miklos, I want you to go upstairs and meet a relative of yours, the Princess Maria Dábas, about whom I told you, when we were coming here."

"I want to see her, Uncle János," Miklos said. "I have read about Imbe Dábas, and how he was executed."

"Do not speak to her of that," the Prince warned, "but she is very anxious to meet you, and hurry, because we must go back soon to the Castle. You will find Newman waiting at the bottom of the stairs to show you the way to the Princess."

Miklos left the Drawing-Room and as soon as he had gone the Prince held out his hands to Forella.

"Listen, my darling," he said, "because there will be a great deal to do here, although I know that Dr Bouvais will make things as easy as possible, I want you to leave immediately for a house I have on the way to Southampton."

Forella looked at him in perplexity, and he said:

"I will join you there later, but I want you to be brave enough to drive there alone and wait for me. Will you do that?"

"You know I will do . . . anything you . . . tell me to do," Forella answered, "but . . . I do not . . . understand."

"I will explain everything," the Prince said, "but it is important that you should not be seen here now, both because you were brave enough to reveal your real name, and also because an accident and a funeral will create gossip, at least locally."

"I understand . . . and I will . . . wait for . . . you."

The Prince raised her hand and kissed it.

"Thank you, my lovely one," he said softly. "Now go and get ready while I explain to the Princess what has occurred. The carriage will be waiting and I will delay everything else until you are gone."

"Thank you . . . thank you," Forella murmured.

He kissed her hand again and she went from the room and up the stairs to her bedroom.

She was not surprised to find that Mrs Newman was already there.

"His Highness says you have to leave at once, M'Lady," she said, "and that's very sad coming on top of the bad news we've had already."

"I am sorry for the 'poor lady'," Forella said quietly.

"We just have to believe that God knows best," Mrs Newman said.

"That is what I thought too," Forella agreed, thinking of how her prayers had been answered.

She changed hurriedly into her travelling clothes and ate a light meal that was brought up to her on a tray.

She found when she went to say goodbye to the Princess that the Prince had already left the Manor to take Miklos to the Castle and then to visit the Chief Constable and explain to him that there had been an accident.

"If you ask me," the Princess said, "it is a merciful release, not only for Gisella, but also, of course, for dear János, although it is certainly not the right thing to say at the moment."

"No . . . of course not," Forella murmured.

"I think we are all feeling apprehensive in case it gets into the newspapers," the Princess went on in a low voice. "If they report who we are, and ask why we are here, anything might happen."

"I am sure the Prince will make certain there is no scandal," Forella answered.

"Why should there be?" the Princess asked. "It was an accident, and although I believe the poor nurses are blaming themselves for leaving her alone, nobody except a complete hypocrite would pretend it was a tragedy."

"I must go . . . Your Highness."

"János told me he was sending you away," the Princess said. "I have loved having you here, and the only thing I regret is that you have not told me your secret, which I think is very unkind of you, considering you know mine!"

"I will tell you everything next time we meet," Forella promised, and the Princess laughed.

"I have a feeling, although perhaps I am being clairvoyant, that that may be sooner than seems possible, and perhaps your circumstances will be different from what they are at the moment."

Forella did not answer.

She knew the Princess's eyes were bright with curiosity as she bent down and kissed her cheek.

"I promise that if I can," she said, "I will write and tell you everything you want to know."

"Then make it soon," the Princess answered, "otherwise I shall die of sheer curiosity!"

Forella laughed.

Then she ran downstairs to find a closed carriage waiting for her outside the door and her trunks with all her pretty new gowns in them stacked up behind.

She noted that the coachman was driving four very fine horses, and as they set off she realised that the carriage in which she was travelling was very light.

She knew they would not take long to complete the

journey and it would be a comfortable one.

It was a strange feeling setting off into the unknown, but because the Prince had arranged it she was not frightened, but merely excited.

It was growing late in the afternoon when the horses turned in at the drive at the end of which was a very attractive house of about the same size as the Manor. But it was of red brick, and proclaimed by its windows and porticoed door that it had been built in the time of Queen Anne.

There were servants waiting to greet her and Forella realised that a groom must have gone ahead to announce their arrival.

The Butler, a younger man than Newman but with the same air of consideration and efficiency, said:

"Welcome, M'Lady!"

This told Forella that she was still to use her mother's family name and as she looked round the very impressive marble hall, she exclaimed:

"What a lovely house this is!"

"His Highness bought it, M'Lady, at the same time as he built his yacht, which he keeps at Southampton. It breaks the journey at exactly the right distance for the horses."

The Butler smiled as he went on:

"His Highness, I'm glad to say, does not care for those new-fangled noisy, dangerous trains as a means of conveyance!"

"Horses are much nicer," Forella replied.

"That's what I thinks, M'Lady," the Butler answered, "and you'll find some very fine horse-flesh in the stables, although I'm sure His Highness'll want to show them to you himself."

Because the Prince was coming to join her, even though he had said it might be late, Forella went upstairs as if in a dream, knowing because she was waiting for him that time would pass slowly.

But it was endowed with a special magic because he was coming to her.

The elderly maid waiting on her suggested that she should rest after her journey, and actually because all the events of the day had been so exhausting, Forella slept.

When she awoke it was to find that it was very much later than she had expected.

She had a bath, and when she had dressed in one of the lovely gowns the Prince had sent her from London she went downstairs expecting to dine alone.

However, when she reached the Hall the Butler said:

"A groom has just arrived, M'Lady, to say that His Highness's on his way, and as I reckon he'll be with us in perhaps an hour's time, I thought you might prefer to wait dinner until His Highness arrives."

"Yes . . . of course," Forella agreed.

She went into the Drawing-Room which was a large room with a high ceiling, and furnished in the same luxurious and tasteful manner which was characteristic of all the Prince's possessions.

Flowers scented the air and windows over which the curtains had not yet been drawn looked out over a garden filled with roses and syringa.

'It is enchanted!' Forella thought.

She felt as if her heart was beating like the tick of the clock and repeating as it did so the Prince's name, over and over again.

*   *   *   *   *

It was a little over an hour later that the door opened.

She was expecting him to appear in his riding-clothes in which he must have travelled very swiftly.

Instead he must have reached the house without

her being aware of it, for he was in evening-dress.

He looked so magnificent and so handsome that she gave a cry of delight not only because he was there, but also because of his appearance.

The door shut behind him, and without thinking, conscious only of her joy, Forella ran towards him.

When she reached him she would have checked herself, but his arms went round her and he held her close and she could feel his heart beating against hers.

"My darling, my sweet!" he said very softly. "I am sorry to have been so long."

"Is . . . everything . . . all . . . right?"

She could hardly say the words and it did not sound like her own voice asking the question.

"Everything," he said. "Come and sit down, and I will tell you all about it."

He took his arms from her and because she knew he expected it of her she walked towards the sofa.

As she sat down the door opened and servants came in with champagne which they poured into crystal glasses, on which were engraved the Prince's insignia.

"Dinner'll be ready in a few minutes, Your Highness," the Butler said as he left the room.

"You must be hungry," the Prince said. "I did not expect you to wait for me."

He was speaking conventionally, and yet what he said was unimportant.

What mattered was the look in his eyes, the deep note in his voice, and the fact that he was so near to her that Forella was trembling with a wild excitement that made her feel as if she was floating on air.

What she ate, what she drank in the Dining-Room and what they said to each other was afterwards impossible to remember.

All she knew was that it seemed as if the angels

were singing overhead, and their music was a love-song that united them as closely as if they were touching each other.

When they returned to the Drawing-Room, and now the curtains were drawn and the candles lit in the chandeliers, the Prince said:

"We have so much to tell each other, but all I really want to say is how beautiful you are, and how much you mean to me."

"Is . . . that true?"

"I think you know without words how much I love you," the Prince said, "and my Hungarian instinct tells me, although you have never said so, that what you feel for me is the beginning of love."

"I do . . . love you!" Forella said, "but I never . . . thought I would be able . . . to tell you . . . so."

"We should have trusted fate, or perhaps God who was looking after us."

He gave a deep sigh before he went on:

"When I knew I must send you away I felt as if I was cutting my heart out of my body, but it was some-thing I had to do."

"Where . . . will you . . . send me . . . now?" Forella asked.

She knew it was a question that had been at the back of her mind all day.

The Prince smiled, and it was as if the whole room was lit with a blazing light.

"I am sending you nowhere, my precious one," he replied. "I am taking you to Hungary after we are married."

"M – married?"

Forella found it hard to say the word, and yet it had been spoken.

"It will not be the marriage which perhaps you had dreamt of with bridesmaids, and a huge Reception,"

the Prince answered. "Because we have to be very
secretive I have arranged that we shall be married
tomorrow morning in the little church here in the
village before we join my yacht at Southampton and
start on our honeymoon."

Forella clasped her hands together.

"I . . . I cannot believe . . . what you are . . .
saying."

"That is, of course," the Prince said, "if you are
willing to marry me."

He paused to say quietly:

"I think, my darling, that we both know that a
force, a power stronger than ourselves, has joined us
together and it would be impossible for us to live
without each other."

"That is . . . true, but I did not . . . think that you
would . . . marry me."

"You are what I have been looking for all my life,"
the Prince said, "and whatever anybody else may
think, I have no intention, having found you, of
losing you."

"That . . . is what I . . . wanted you to say," she
answered.

"But please . . . you are quite certain that I am the
. . . right person . . . the right sort of wife . . . and I
shall not . . . fail you?"

The Prince gave a laugh that was one of sheer
happiness.

"I am quite, quite certain," he said. "It is going to
take a very long time, perhaps an eternity, to
persuade you of how much I love you and how certain
I am that you are the wife who was born just for me
and that we can never lose each other again – never!"

The way he spoke was very moving.

Then gently he put his arms around Forella and
drew her close to him. He looked down at her for a

long moment.

"How can you be so perfect, so exquisite," he asked, "that I find it hard even when I am touching you to believe that you are real?"

He did not wait for her to reply.

His lips came down on hers and she knew at the touch of them that this was what she had been longing and aching for ever since she had realised that she loved him.

At first his mouth was very gentle, then as he felt her whole body melt into his and her lips surrendered themselves completely to him, his kiss became more insistent, more demanding and very much more possessive.

He held her closer and still closer until she felt a wild rapture sweep through her.

It moved from her breast into her throat and from her throat into her lips where the fire that seemed to come from the Prince ignited a fire within her too.

It was so ecstatic that she could hardly believe it was actually happening.

Then as he kissed her and went on kissing her she could no longer think.

She could only feel that he had carried her up into a Heaven where they were alone, and they touched the Divine.

When at last the Prince raised his head Forella managed to say incoherently:

"I . . . love . . . you . . . I love . . . you! Can this . . . really be . . . happening? I think I must be . . . dreaming!"

"Then I am dreaming, too," the Prince said, "but our dreams have come true. I have found you and, my precious, I have been so desperately afraid, because I was not free to ask you to be my wife, that I would lose you."

She knew by the way he spoke that it had been a very real fear.

She thought how she had felt in despair that there were so many beautiful women in his life that he would have no time for her.

Then she knew that their love was different from anything they might feel or think about other people, and as the Prince had said, they were one person.

He was looking into her eyes and as if he knew what she was thinking, he said:

"My darling, my bride, my heart, my soul, and without exception, the most perfect rider I have ever seen!"

Because it was so far from what she had expected him to say, Forella gave a little gurgling laugh.

"Am I really a . . . good rider?" she asked.

"Of course," he replied, "and we will ride together on horses which I believe are the best in the world, and certainly the most spirited and very, very wild."

Forella drew in her breath as she said:

"It all sounds very wonderful . . . but you know the only thing that really . . . matters is that . . . you will be there. I did not want to go to Hungary when you said you would . . . send me there because it meant leaving you behind."

"That is something you will never do in the future," the Prince said. "Oh, my darling, I never knew I could find such happiness so unexpectedly after so many years of feeling alone even in the midst of a crowd."

Because she suddenly felt protective towards him Forella reached up to touch his cheek with her hand.

"I will never . . . let you be . . . alone again," she said, "and I want . . . more than anything . . . else in the world . . . to give you . . . a son."

The Prince looked at her as if he could hardly

believe what she had said.

Then without replying he kissed her passionately, demandingly and now rather differently.

She knew that she had excited him, and at the same time she had offered him what he longed for, and she could fill his life as no other women had ever been able to do.

"I love you . . . I . . . love you!" she said because there were no other words to express her feelings.

"And I adore you!" the Prince said. "Tomorrow, my darling, you will be mine, and there will be no more problems, no more unhappiness."

He paused and added:

"And no more lonely nights of lying awake and thinking about you, knowing there was no possible way in which I could make you mine."

The passion in his voice was very moving and as he felt a little tremor go through her he said:

"I have so much to teach you, my precious love, so much to awaken in your heart, your mind and your beautiful body, which is very Hungarian."

Forella knew what he meant and gave a little laugh of sheer happiness.

Then he was kissing her again, and it was impossible to think of anything except that nothing mattered in the future except that he should be there.

She was his, as he was hers, for all eternity.

Now that they were together, no one could divide them or spoil their love which filled the whole world and had been given to them by God.

Barbara Cartland

Barbara Cartland is one of Britain's bestselling romantic novelists and the following titles from her are available from Arrow. You can buy them from your local bookshop or newsagent, or you can order them direct through the post. Just tick the titles you require and complete the form below.

☐	CAUGHT BY LOVE	£1.00
☐	EXPLOSION OF LOVE	£1.00
☐	THE HEART OF THE CLAN	95p
☐	IN THE ARMS OF LOVE	£1.25
☐	THE JUDGEMENT OF LOVE	£1.00
☐	KISS OF LOVE	£1.10
☐	LOVE IS INNOCENT	£1.00
☐	LOVE LEAVES AT MIDNIGHT	£1.00
☐	LUCIFER AND THE ANGEL	£1.00
☐	THE NAKED BATTLE	£1.00
☐	ONLY LOVE	£1.00
☐	PURE AND UNTOUCHED	£1.00
☐	RIDING TO THE MOON	£1.25
☐	THE TREASURE IS LOVE	£1.00

Postage _____

Total _____

ARROW BOOKS, BOOKSERVICE BY POST, PO BOX 29, DOUGLAS, ISLE OF MAN, BRITISH ISLES

Please enclose a cheque or postal order made out to Arrow Books Limited for the amount due including 15p per book for postage and packing for orders both within the UK and overseas.

Please print clearly

NAME ....

ADDRESS ....

....

Whilst every effort is made to keep prices down and to keep popular books in print, Arrow Books cannot guarantee that prices will be the same as those advertised here or that the books will be available.